A few months ago, this would have been science fiction. We were living in Serenity, 100 percent convinced it was the best place on earth. Even Malik, who complained about how boring it was, was just blustering when he talked about leaving one day. What little we knew about the outside world centered around the fact that we didn't want to go there—it was lawless; it was dirty; it was horrible.

Now we're right smack dab in the middle of that world, and most of the lawless, dirty, and horrible things we've seen here are being done by *us*. And don't think it doesn't haunt us that this makes perfect sense. After all, we're supposed to be exact copies of some of the worst criminals the human race has to offer.

Haunting or not, though, we don't have time to worry that we might be living up to the evil in our DNA. We have to get Amber back. Period.

Also by Gordon Korman

Masterminds

Ungifted

Pop

MASTERMINDS

CRIMINAL DESTINY

GORDON KORMAN

BALZER + BRAY
An Imprint of Harper Collins*Publishers*

For Daisy Korman, Theatrical Mastermind

Balzer + Bray is an imprint of HarperCollins Publishers.

Masterminds: Criminal Destiny

For information address HarperCollins Children's Books, a division of HarperCollins Publishers, 195 Broadway, New York, NY 10007.
www.harpercollinschildrens.com

Library of Congress Control Number: 2015015706
ISBN 978-0-06-230003-4

17 18 19 20 CG/OPM 10 9 8 7 6 5 4 3 2

❖

First paperback edition, 2017

1

ELI FRIEDEN

"I see your taco and raise you half a cheeseburger."

I peer at my cards. I've got a pair of kings and a pair of eights. It's a pretty good hand, I think. Then again, I only learned the rules of poker twenty minutes ago. I'm from Serenity, New Mexico, where nobody plays poker because it's gambling.

Trust me, that's far from the weirdest thing about the place.

"Come on, Eli. In or out?" Randy Hardaway demands. He's from Serenity, too, but he's been here in the real world for a couple of months already, so he knows a lot more than I do about things like poker.

The third player, Malik Bruder, tosses his cards on the carpet. "Forget it. I quit."

"You're supposed to say *I fold*," Randy corrects.

"Whatever. Let's eat. I'm starving."

"It's not food, it's our stakes," Randy insists. "If we eat it now, we've got nothing to bet with. When the game's over it can be food again."

I laugh. "But by then you'll have won it all."

"And if I'm in a good mood, I might even consider sharing it with you. Now let's play."

With a plastic knife, I saw off a piece of my own burger and place it in the Styrofoam takeout container that's serving as the pot. "Fine," I say, turning my cards over. "I have two pairs."

"Not good enough," Randy cackles, revealing his own hand: three sixes. "You guys are such suckers! It's like you just graduated kindergarten yesterday."

"Ha!" Malik snorts. "Kindergarten is like NYC compared to where we just blasted out of."

Malik isn't even exaggerating about the "blasted out" part. We didn't just leave Serenity; we escaped from it on a speeding truck. It would be a great story, except that one of us—a kid named Hector—didn't make it.

There's a knock at the door of Randy's room—the secret knock, which means Malik and I don't have to fight over who gets to hide under the bed and who has to squeeze into the jam-packed closet. We're not supposed to be at McNally Academy, Randy's boarding school. It's just the place we came to after we escaped. Randy was the only person we knew on the outside. He was sent away to school because he was getting too close to the truth about how our "perfect community" was a big lie.

The door opens to admit Randy's roommate, Kevin, and another kid. The two of them are weighed down with bags and Styrofoam containers. "Good news—we got leftover pizza and some fried chicken—" Kevin's eyes fall on the smorgasbord of food serving as poker stakes. "Thanks a lot. We risk our necks raiding the cafeteria to feed your poor starving runaway friends, and you're using it to gamble with!"

"We'll eat it—eventually," Randy explains. "And don't forget we need some for the girls."

I stand up. "We should take it over to them now. They're probably pretty hungry."

"I'll go with you," Malik decides. "Maybe *they'll* feed me. And anyway, my mother always told me not to play with my food."

He stops short, and I can tell he's thinking about home. He loved his parents, especially his mom, who babied him and treated him like a royal prince. That's not a problem I have. There was only my dad, and he turned out to be the ringleader of all of Project Osiris—him and this billionaire lady none of us have ever met.

Not that any of our parents were *real* parents—you know, in the biological sense. What we are, actually, is clones—part of a twisted, secret experiment. The whole town of Serenity was created just for Project Osiris. We were guinea pigs, lab rats. That's why we had to run away. It was our only chance at having actual lives.

Randy isn't one of the clones, but in a way, his life revolved around Project Osiris every bit as much as ours. When he got overly curious about why some of us were "special," his own parents—*real* parents—chose to banish him to McNally rather than risk contaminating the experiment. That has to hurt.

Nobody at McNally knows that besides Randy. And even he doesn't have the whole story. He knows we're clones; what he doesn't know is who we're cloned *from.*

I wish I didn't.

We peer out the door to make sure the coast is clear.

"We're good to go—" Malik begins.

Whump! The noise isn't that loud, but it's almost like a mini-earthquake. The building seems to resettle on its foundation.

Kevin grabs the two of us, hauls us back into the room, slams the door, and locks it.

Malik, who's a big guy and not used to being manhandled, dusts himself off, his jaw stuck out.

"What was that?" I ask, a little shaken.

Randy leads me to the window and we peek through the venetian blinds out to the front drive. A huge flag lies on the grass where no flag should ever be. Two moving bumps scramble out and begin frantically trying to fold the billowing silk.

"This happens at least twice a week," Randy explains. "The flag's gigantic, and the pulley's broken, so the littler kids can't handle it."

"That's fascinating," drawls Malik. "And I should care about this because . . . ?"

The answer to that becomes apparent when a short, fat man in a suit comes running over from the administration building, waving his arms. We can't make out his words, but it's pretty clear that he's chewing out the kids for letting the flag touch the ground, which is a serious no-no.

"That's the headmaster, Mr. Ross," Kevin supplies.

And if we were on our way to the girls' dorm, we'd be passing twenty feet in front of him.

"Just give him a few more minutes to go through the

usual song and dance," Randy soothes. "He's not a bad guy, if you don't mind windbags. Reminds me of your old man a little bit."

I almost tell him what he already knows—that my old man *is* a bad guy, technically a mad scientist. But I can't say that in front of Kevin.

Eventually, the lecture is over and the flag gets folded up and put away for the night. When Mr. Ross goes back to the administration building, Malik and I gather up our food and hustle over to the girls' dormitory.

We catch a couple of inquisitive looks from students on the way. According to Randy, there are rumors circulating about us: we're new arrivals nobody's had a chance to meet yet; we're friends and/or cousins on break from a year-round school; we're foreign exchange students. That last one is my favorite, since there isn't a country on earth that's as foreign as Serenity, New Mexico. Luckily, the kids here are too wrapped up in their own lives to worry about us all that much, one way or the other.

The people actually hiding us have the explanation closest to reality. Randy told them we're runaways from his backward hometown. It's the truth—with a few important details left out.

At room 122 I give the secret knock.

No one answers.

I knock again, louder this time. There are some scrambling sounds and the door opens a crack.

"We've got food," Malik says impatiently. "You have three seconds to let us in, or I eat your share."

Tori Pritel ushers us inside. This room is smaller than Randy's, but nicer, with better furniture and satellite TV. It belongs to McNally Academy's nurse, who's on an exchange program at a school in Maryland for the next three weeks.

The fourth member of our group, Amber Laska, doesn't even look up. She's completely engrossed in a news broadcast. We've all been media-obsessed since leaving Serenity. Our TV, radio, and even internet were strictly controlled by Project Osiris. Any information about crime or conflict or violence was kept from us. Even the history we were taught left out unpleasant details like wars and revolutions. The only reason we knew about lying was so we could be told that nobody from Serenity ever did it. There were no secrets in Serenity—except for the fact that the whole town was a secret. And we weren't supposed to find out about that.

So here we are, four escaped clones in the middle of a world that is an absolute mystery to us. We're kind of protected at McNally, but we can't stay much longer. Sooner or later, the rumors about us are going to reach the teachers.

We spread our donated food for a picnic on the carpet. Malik picks a stethoscope up off the floor and holds it dangling by an earpiece. "What's this for?"

"It must belong to the nurse," Tori replies. "But we've been using it to listen in on the room next door."

"Spying on the neighbors." Malik clucks disapprovingly. "Not very Serenity-like. This is going to bring down your grade in Contentment class."

She flushes. "It's not spying. We're just trying to get a sense of what real kids talk about."

"And?" I prompt.

"There's a lot of discussion about a person called the Bachelor. I think he might be in the government. Also Starbucks—that's a restaurant in Pueblo. It must be superfancy, because all the things you can order have these long foreign names. Oh—and zombies." She shrugs. "We haven't figured out what those are yet. Jewelry, maybe."

"Sounds like some kind of earrings," Malik suggests without much interest. "Come on, let's eat."

We dig in. Eventually, the smell of lukewarm pizza gets through to Amber and she joins us.

"I just saw a report," she fumes between hungry bites, "about people who get sick but they can't see doctors because they can't afford it! In what universe is that allowed to happen?"

"This one," I tell her honestly. "And it's probably not the hardest thing we're going to have to get used to."

"Well, that's *wrong*!" she insists, getting louder.

"Shhh!" Tori cautions. "We're supposed to be *hiding*."

"But in Serenity—"

"Happy Valley was never a real place," Malik interrupts, using his pet name for our former hometown. "It was a big petri dish, only more boring. And we were the germs they were growing in it."

Basically, Project Osiris is a scientific study to determine if terrible people are born terrible, or if their environments make them that way. Would evil kids raised in an isolated community where nothing bad ever happens still grow up to be evil?

The problem is this: Where do you get evil *babies*? My "father," Felix Frieden—actually, Hammerstrom—came up with a solution that's as awful as it is ingenious: you *clone* them—from evil *adults*.

Project Osiris took DNA from some of the worst criminal masterminds in the prison system and created eleven clones—the four of us, poor Hector, and six others still in Serenity. If a sweet, wholesome upbringing can turn the scum of the earth into ordinary citizens, it proves that there are no bad people, only bad environments.

We were never supposed to find out the truth about ourselves. Bad enough the only parents we've ever known turn out to be the scientists who did this to us. Then there's the little detail that we are exact copies of some of the most depraved criminals ever.

One of us—one of the boys, anyway—is cloned from Bartholomew Glen, the notorious Crossword Killer. It's impossible to be sure which. The pictures of him on the internet show a middle-aged inmate with a shaved head, wide staring eyes, and a crazed expression. None of us look like him—or maybe we all do. Fast-forward a few decades and one of us will for sure, which is pretty scary. As for the others, we can't even guess who they're cloned from, which is scarier still.

The next few moments are devoted to the kind of serious eating perfected by Malik. Even Amber, who's always on a diet, is double-fisting pizza slices. It's a small thing, but it shows that we've shifted into Fugitive Mode. Fugitives eat like they don't know where their next meal will come from, because they don't. When we first got to McNally, the stash of jellybeans hidden in Randy's underwear drawer was the first food we'd seen in nearly two days.

"This is great," Malik mumbles, his mouth full.

"It isn't, you know," Tori says thoughtfully. "We just *need* it more. I'd give anything for Steve's jalapeño meatloaf right now." She calls her dad by his first name—the scientist she thought was her dad, I mean.

Malik cocks an eyebrow at her. "Having second thoughts, Torific?"

She glares back. "We left because we had no choice—we all get that. It doesn't change the fact that I miss my parents."

Malik won't let it drop. "The only parents we have are eyedroppers and test tubes."

"Leave her alone, Malik," Amber snaps. "You know what she means."

I speak up. "This is pointless, you guys. Yeah, we miss certain things. But if any of us got the chance to go back home, no questions asked, who'd take it?"

Dead silence.

"But what are we going to *do*?" asks Tori. "I mean, we can't stay here forever. Sooner or later, the teachers who run this place are bound to notice they've picked up a few extra kids."

Malik snorts. "I didn't bust out of Happy Valley to hang out in a place just as lame. I'm going to see the world."

Amber makes a face. "That's all we are now? Tourists?"

"You've got a better idea?"

"Justice!" she exclaims. "It's so simple. What happened in Serenity is a *crime*. We need to go to the police and get our so-called parents arrested for what they did to us."

"Police!" Malik spits. "The only police we've ever known are the Purple People Eaters, and how much justice did they ever dish out?" He's talking about the Surety, Serenity's police force, who are really just the enforcers for Project Osiris. "You think the cops are any different? They could hand us right back to the Purples. Or arrest us for being clones. For all we know, that's against the law. And wait till they figure out who we're clones *of*."

I have to agree. "It's complicated. We can't go to the police until we know more about how things work in the outside world."

"And don't forget there are six others like us still in Serenity," Tori puts in. "They deserve a chance at a real life every bit as much as we do."

"But no pressure," adds Malik sarcastically.

There is a sharp rap at the door, and everyone freezes. It's not the secret knock.

"Is somebody there?" calls an adult voice.

Then we hear the sound of a key in the lock.

We're galvanized into action. Tori disappears into the closet with what's left of the pizza. Amber scoots under the bed with the rest of the food. I try to roll under there too, but Malik beats me to it, and I bounce off his bulky form. The doorknob turns, and there I am, still out in the open. The thought that I escaped from Serenity only to be caught in a random dorm inspection lends my feet wings. I literally fly to the bathroom, and dive into the tub, pulling the curtain closed.

There are footsteps, and the teacher's voice again: "I could have sworn I heard someone in here." The door opens and closes. The footsteps die away in the corridor.

And a moment later, the four of us are staring at each other. The crisis is over as quickly as it began. But the feeling of being close to disaster has not yet gone away.

Maybe it never will.

2

AMBER LASKA

I'm running through the woods, the leafy branches slapping at my face, my sneakers pounding against the uneven ground.

I know what you're thinking. Too risky. I get that. If any adult sees me, we're all toast.

That's why I'm exercising under the cover of the trees. This brings its own set of hazards, though. If I trip on a tree root and break my ankle, everything we're trying to do instantly becomes ten times harder. But how can I stay cooped up in that room any longer? Especially when I've worked so hard with diet and exercise to achieve my goal weight.

I used to start each morning by making a to-do list of everything I needed to accomplish that day. I wouldn't have to think about how much time to spend practicing ballet; it would be right there on the list: *Practice ballet—1.5 hours.* I'd know exactly how long to spend on each homework assignment—my "mom" was our teacher, and it wouldn't do for her daughter to be anything less than perfect. If I was going over to Tori's to swim or hang out, the list would say how long I could do that too. I was in complete control of my life.

Since we left Serenity—I can't believe it was only three days ago—I've become list-proof. You can't plan anything when you're on the run. All you can do is react to what happens to you, and do your best to stay free. Ballet and piano and water polo and studying—all the things that defined me before—now take a backseat to survival.

I miss my lists. Even though they don't really work anymore, I still see them in my mind as they might apply to my current situation:

THINGS TO DO TODAY (UNPRIORITIZED)

- Run in woods (45 minutes)–watch out for roots!
- Learn about outside world (ongoing)
- Control rage (difficult but necessary)
- Cut down on the pizza!!!

That's another reason I have to exercise. Doesn't the McNally cafeteria serve anything healthy? Or is the problem that Randy and his friends never met a vegetable they didn't hate? Not that beggars can be choosers, of course.

Randy thought I was crazy when I peppered him with questions about the campus and schedule, but I needed to plot a running route where no teacher would ever look for me. I time myself to finish when classes are changing and it's no problem for me to melt into the crowd of kids. One thing about life outside Serenity—you see so many random faces that you can't think too much about any of them.

Monitoring my heart rate with a finger on my throat, I join the parade of girls crowding into the dormitory. I have to remind myself that the inquisitive glances coming my way are saying "Who's that?" not "Clone alert! Clone alert!" Nobody knows about that except Randy. I wonder what they'd think if they did. I'm not even sure how *I* feel about it—just that I feel it a lot.

Then I'm in the safety of the nurse's room. Tori's got the stethoscope on, the probe pressed to the wall. I shoot her the high sign that, no, I haven't been followed.

She beckons me over.

I don't really share Tori's obsession with listening in on the girls next door. The things that are important to them seem shallow and borderline stupid—like which companies manufacture their clothes, or which guys at McNally are "hot." Trust me, none of the guys here are hot the way *they* mean it—as in good-looking. At one point, I could have sworn they were talking about Malik, if you can believe such a thing! It's almost enough to make me want to go back to Serenity.

Almost.

Tori removes one earpiece and extends it to me. We have to get really close to listen in together, but that's not unusual for Tori and me. We've been best friends practically since birth.

The girls next door are going on and on about necklaces they bought on a class trip to a Native American art gallery in Pueblo that morning.

I roll my eyes and whisper, "You'd think they're talking about a cure for cancer or something."

Tori cuts me off with an urgent finger to her lips. That's when one of the girls mentions ". . . those cops in the weird purple uniforms."

My eyes meet Tori's. Purple uniforms? I don't like the sound of that.

"They must be from the Never-Never-Land Police Department," the other girl giggles.

"What color do the Pueblo cops wear?" I ask in a low voice.

We rush to the nurse's computer and call up the website of the Pueblo PD. A smiling officer in a jet-black uniform appears on the screen. There's no way anyone could mistake it for purple.

Only one kind of "cop" wears purple.

It's bad news. Worse than bad. There could be only one reason for a Purple People Eater in Pueblo, Colorado—Project Osiris has put two and two together and played a hunch that the four of us would have come to Randy. The more I consider it, the more obvious it seems.

"We have to tell the guys," I decide. Compared to Serenity, Pueblo seems gigantic. But it isn't so big that the Purples will have much trouble finding McNally Academy once they start nosing around.

And getting caught isn't an option. One thing all four of us understand is that escaping Serenity is something we will only ever have one chance to do. If we're dragged back, they'll put cameras on us while we sleep, and brainwash us into forgetting Project Osiris ever existed. The only reason we got away the first time was that they didn't know that we were learning the truth about ourselves. If they get their hands on us this time, we'll never be free again. So far, freedom hasn't been that great. But it still beats what we've come from.

We're out of the building, running for the Hayden dorm, where the boys are staying.

We bust into Randy's room without any kind of knock, secret or otherwise.

"The Purples are onto us!" I bark. "A couple of girls spotted one in town!"

"That explains the call!" Randy says gravely.

"What call?" asks Tori.

"My parents called an hour ago," he explains. "They were asking all kinds of nosy questions. And they told me not to do anything stupid. Like they don't know I'm *always* doing something stupid!"

Eli's on his feet. "The message was don't get between us and the Purples. That means things will get rough if we don't go along with them."

"You think they're ready to start breaking heads?" Randy asks, alarmed.

Malik picks up a lacrosse stick leaning against the bookcase. "Ours aren't the only heads that can break."

Tori is practical. "If you go up against a trained commando, you're going to lose. There's only one thing for us to do, and that's escape."

"Using what?" Malik challenges. "Our jet-packs?"

"There's a bus that goes into Pueblo," Randy supplies. "You can catch it at the bottom of the hill at the end of the main drive." He turns to Eli. "I guess this reunion's going to be shorter than we expected."

Eli is pale, but determined. "We'll never forget what you did for us, man. I—I just wish things were different."

They shake hands, but that's all the ceremony we've got time for.

We're just about to head out of the room when, plain as day through the front window, we see a black SUV pull up the circular drive and stop between the two dorms. The doors open, and there they are. Our worst nightmares: the Surety with their purple uniforms and wine-colored berets.

"We're too late!" Eli moans.

I find my eyes traveling to Malik's lacrosse stick. Win or lose, I'm not going down without a fight. To my surprise, I'm almost relishing the idea. For the first time ever, I think of the criminal I'm cloned from, languishing in a prison cell somewhere. This must be her impulse, not mine. But it's there all the same. What am I turning into?

No. Wrong question. I've always been this. I just didn't know it until recently.

"We need cover," Tori says, her voice strangely calm.

Malik is freaking out. "There's no cover! Either we go out and get spotted, or they come in after us! Those are the choices—bad and worse!"

In answer, Tori runs out of the room and pulls the fire alarm. Instantly, the Hayden dorm resounds with a blaring siren. Doors are flung wide, and the halls fill with students heading for the exits. We all realize it at the same time. *This* is Tori's cover—hundreds of other kids, all milling around in the general confusion. I wish I'd thought of it.

"Follow me!" cries Randy, leading us into the throng.

Outside the dorm, the crowd surges. It reminds me of something my mother taught us in science—a giant amoeba. We try to stay near the center of it, its nucleus. Kids are spilling out of the other dorm, and faculty members are running over from the main building to investigate the alarm.

Stay calm, Amber, I advise myself.

I get a fresh stab of fear when I spot my first Purple—the one that we used to call Rump L. Stiltskin. He's scanning the crowd, peering into faces. That has to be good news. It means the enemy hasn't spotted us yet.

You know how people talk about walking tall? We walk short, keeping to the center of the crowd. I identify another Purple—Baron Vladimir von Horseteeth. And there's

Bryan Delaney, the husband of our water polo coach. We shuffle along, but the odds are stacked against us. The Purples know us so well. Some of them have been watching us since the day we were born.

I have no idea how we think we're going to get away. Plan A is out of the question. No way can we go to the bottom of the hill and wait for a bus now. And there never was a Plan B. There's no to-do list for this situation.

Rump L. Stiltskin points. "There!" At first I think he's found me, but no—it's Tori in his sights. She keeps on walking for a minute. I have no idea how. I would have been frozen like a deer in headlights.

They start closing in. Five Purples—I see them all now, spaced around the students like the points of a star. Kids begin to scatter. Purple uniforms or no, the Surety look like they mean business.

And then Tori's running. She breaks from the mass, and the Purples fall in behind her. That's how quickly it turns into a chase. I resist the impulse to run to her. It wouldn't do any good. And, let's face it, I'm every bit as much a target as she is. Moving with speed fueled by raw desperation, Tori sprints across the quad, and up onto the lawn. She's a good athlete, but her pursuers are gaining on her. They close the gap to thirty feet. It's only a matter of time before her break for freedom ends in disaster.

As she passes by the main flagpole, Eli scrambles out from the milling students and unwraps the flag rope from the cleat that holds it in place. All at once, the crank is spinning, and a dark shadow descends from above.

Just as the five Purples pass by the pole, the huge flag flops down on them. The broad, heavy silk lands with such speed and force that it flattens them in their tracks. They struggle against the fabric, arms and legs growing ever more tangled as they flail.

The door of the SUV is thrown open, and the driver emerges. It's Secret Agent Man, one of the older Purples. He's torn for an instant. Should he go after Tori, or make an effort to free his fellow Surety from the fallen flag? Before he can come to a decision, Malik barrels out from a group of students and makes a bull run at him.

Malik crashes headfirst into the Purple's midsection. The guy's a trained security guard, but the element of surprise knocks him backward on his butt.

We're all running to help Malik when I see it: the SUV is right there on the driveway, key in the ignition, idling. Not only is it a possible means of escape—it's our only one. I have no idea how to drive a car, but Eli sort of does. He drove us out of Serenity in a stolen truck piled high with orange traffic cones.

The other Purples have thrown off the flag, and are pounding our way. Secret Agent Man is gaining the upper hand in his battle with Malik. We have to act *now*!

I hurl myself in through the open driver door, and scramble to the passenger side to make room for Eli at the wheel. Tori jumps in the back, terrified and hyperventilating.

Eli stares at the dashboard. "This isn't the same as the cone truck!"

"*Drive!*" I never knew I could scream that loud.

It does the trick because Eli throws the car in gear, and climbs the curb onto the lawn. Secret Agent Man gets Malik in a headlock. And the next thing he knows, his own car is coming at him, chewing up turf. The rear door swings open, catching him in the side of the head.

Nice shot, Tori!

It literally peels him off Malik, who hits the ground, bounces up, and hurls himself into the backseat, flattening Tori.

Eli stomps on the gas, and we thump back onto the driveway. For a moment, I spot the other five Purples in the side mirror, running full out, chasing us. Eli speeds up, and we leave them in the dust. That's our last view of the McNally campus as we start down the hill—cheering, excited kids, and six Purple People Eaters, flat-footed and stranded.

"Maniac!" Malik gasps. "You could have run me down!"

Eli is hunched over the wheel, concentrating on his steering in the manner of a very early beginner. "You think I was aiming for you?"

"There's no aiming in your driving! You just grip it and rip it!"

"Shut up, Malik!" I snap over the seat. "Where would you rather be—in here with us, or back there with them?"

Malik's anger melts away. We're all quiet, thinking about what almost happened.

A new voice breaks the silence, one that doesn't belong to any of the four of us.

"What's your status? Have you got them? Over."

We're all struck dumb until I notice the two-way radio built into the dashboard. But who's calling? Surely not the six we left back at McNally. They know their status. Are there other Purples around?

"Please respond. We see you've left the campus. Repeat: Do you have them? Over."

"How do they know where we are?" whispers Tori. "Are we being followed?"

"No, not followed." I recognize the rhythmic clatter behind the voice over the radio. I roll down my window and stick my head out. There's a helicopter directly overhead—the Purples' helicopter. "The chopper," I conclude.

Eli presses down on the accelerator, and the SUV speeds up. Its wheels bite at the gravel of the soft shoulder as he struggles with the steering on the winding road.

"Slow down!" Tori urges. "You'll get us all killed!"

"It's not like this thing can outrun a chopper anyway," Malik adds in a resigned tone.

"As long as they're up there and we're down here, we're not caught yet," Eli argues stubbornly.

As we reach the bottom of the hill and swerve onto the main road, we're passed by a fire truck heading up toward the school, siren wailing. It already seems like hours ago that Tori pulled the fire alarm. But the truth is it's only been a couple of minutes. Time slows down when you're running for your life.

The radio crackles as the chopper asks about our status once again. Only this time there's a furious response from one of the Purples we left behind at McNally. *"We're still at the school! The kids took off with our car!"*

There's a stunned silence, then, *"Sorry, I didn't catch that. Repeat your status. Over."*

Malik reaches up from the backseat, pushes the button on the radio, and barks, "Our status is 'leaving'! What are you—blind?"

After a long, static-filled pause, the voice from the chopper says, *"Be reasonable, kids. We're directly above you. There's no way you can escape."*

The unfairness of that really gets to me. "Like they have the right to tell us what's reasonable!" I scoff. "The people who thought it was a great idea to clone criminals!"

Malik presses the button again. "So land on our roof and arrest us!"

"Cut it out," Eli says peevishly. "I'm having enough trouble as it is, keeping this thing on the road."

Without warning, Tori stretches over Eli, clamps a hand on the wheel, and wrenches it to the right. The SUV swerves off the road, lurches over some scrub brush, and bumps up onto pavement again, a narrow curved ramp. We whiz past a sign:

I-25 NORTH—DENVER

"What did you do that for?" Eli's voice is an octave higher than usual.

"This is our route," Tori insists.

"Our route?" Malik echoes. "We don't have a route! We don't know where we're going!"

Tori points. "Look how crowded that road is. It must be a highway. We have to blend in with a lot of other cars if we want to lose that chopper."

She's right. The strip we're about to merge onto is humming with more cars and trucks than we've ever seen in our lives, all moving at high speeds.

Eli inserts the SUV into the nearest lane of traffic, his shoulders up around his ears, like he's bracing himself to get hit by another vehicle. There's no accident, but a chorus of horns greets our arrival, and keeps on greeting as dozens of cars stream around us.

I watch the parade of angry faces, many accompanied by rude gestures. I should be insulted, but really, I'm just fascinated. So this is the real world—infinite faces, infinite moods, infinite speeds, hurry, hurry, hurry. The first word that comes to mind is *messy*. There doesn't seem to be any order out here. It's just a clash of everybody doing their own thing, at the same time, in the same space. But it's also messy the way a forest is messy, with its thousands of species of plant life, growing every which way. The sheer chaos of it is what makes it cool.

Eventually, Eli figures out that he needs to match the

speed of the other cars. The horns and angry shouts begin to fade away. One problem solved, crossed off my mental list.

Only nine hundred to go.

For a guy who taught himself how to drive on Xbox, Eli's doing a pretty good job. We continue on that way for about an hour, Malik watching through the sunroof, following every move the chopper makes overhead.

"It's still up there, in case anybody's interested," he reports. "If they're planning on losing us, they need to hurry up and do it."

"They're not going to lose us," says Eli grimly. "They're trained trackers. They'll follow us to the ends of the earth."

Tori looks thoughtful. "We have to ditch the SUV."

"And do what?" Malik returns. "Jog down the center line of the highway?"

"We could make a break for the woods," I suggest. "A chopper can't land there."

Eli nixes that idea. "Then we'd be stranding ourselves. They could take their time, and come and get us at their leisure."

"Have you guys been seeing these signs along the highway?" Tori puts in. "'Beat the Traffic—Ditch Your Car'?"

Malik is too keyed up to be patient. "If it doesn't get that helicopter off our necks, why do I care about this?"

"Because we're looking for a place to ditch our car, dummy," I explain.

"No, we aren't," he reasons. "There are Purples up there! The minute we're on foot, they'll land the chopper and grab us."

"Not if we're somewhere so big and crowded that they can't find us," Tori reasons.

I haven't noticed any of the signs before, but now that I'm looking, they're every couple of miles. *Denver South Park-n-Ride.* I don't know what it is, but it sounds big.

We notice the parking lot first—acres upon acres of vehicles, far more than we've ever seen in our lives. Unless the Purple People Eaters are ready to bring their helicopter on top of somebody's station wagon or SUV, they won't be able to get within half a mile of us.

"Go!" Tori urges.

Eli's already veering onto the exit ramp, two packed lanes that veer off and cloverleaf over the highway. At the center of the sea of cars is a sprawling terminal building. Dozens of buses stand along it, loading up. The instant a full one drives off, another arrives to take its place. The stream of passengers never slows.

"Whoa!" I breathe. "I didn't think there were this many people in the world!"

"Leave the car over there," Tori instructs Eli. "We've got a bus to catch."

"A bus to where?" Malik asks.

"It doesn't matter so long as the Purples don't see which one it is."

Eli does a terrible job parking the SUV, leaving it at an angle, taking up two spaces. We barely notice. We jump out and run for the buses, keeping our heads low, trying to blend in with the crowd. It's more city noise than I ever experienced in my life—the whiz of cars passing on the highway, the strain of large bus engines, the chatter of so many conversations blending into a background roar. And, yes, the rotor of the chopper still hovering overhead.

"Follow me," Tori hisses.

Staying close, but not together, we push our way into a line, drawing annoyed stares from the other passengers. We wait until we're almost at the entrance before she leads us into another line, and then a third, this one partially obscured by a shelter.

Soon the chopper overhead is going back and forth across the Park-n-Ride, which is how we know they've lost us. It's much easier to keep track of a big black SUV than four tiny heads, bobbing amid thousands of others. That's our cue to board the nearest bus.

The driver is collecting tickets, but a few people pay with cash. A small sign says the fare is four dollars. It's a bargain, I decide. To get away from those Purple People Eaters, we'd gladly hand over every cent we have.

We find seats wherever we can, hunker down, and wait for departure.

Several minutes later, when the bus pulls out and merges onto the highway, the chopper is still searching for us over the parking lot.

My eyes meet Tori's, and I offer an approving nod. If we've truly gotten away, it's thanks to her.

For the first time, I notice the video display behind the driver. It announces our destination: *Denver: Downtown Terminal.*

"Denver," I say aloud, as if getting used to the idea. "I'm going to Denver."

My seatmate, an older lady, gives me an odd look. "I hope you knew where we were going before you got on the bus." Her eyes narrow a little. "How old are you, dear?"

Whoops. A revised to-do list appears in my mind.

THINGS TO DO TODAY (ABSOLUTELY PRIORITIZED)

- Be careful what you say—and who you say it to!

"Sixteen," I reply airily. "I'm meeting some friends to do research for a school project."

Funny. Back in Serenity, they taught us that lying was just about the worst thing you could ever do.

I wonder how I got so good at it.

3

MALIK BRUDER

Well, it finally happened. I am one million percent out of Happy Valley.

The bus depot in Denver has to be the most un-Serenity place on the face of the earth. First off, it's packed. The entire population of Happy Valley must go by every thirty seconds. And they're not just going by. They're moving in about a thousand different directions, bumping into each other, bouncing off, pushing, sidestepping, rushing, arguing, muttering, and cursing under their breath. Everyone is either impatient, or angry, or both. There are a few small kids, and they're all crying. Announcements are blaring over a PA system, in English and Spanish, I think. It's impossible to be sure. The speakers are crackling and buzzing, and you can't make out any of it. Somebody has spray-painted stuff on the walls, but it's too messy to read. There's garbage all over the floor, including right near the garbage can. And the smell! It's a combination of sweaty laundry, wet newspaper, and a bathroom right before it gets cleaned.

I love this place.

So of course, Tori is the polar opposite. "This is *horrible*! How do people live like this?"

"Nobody *lives* here," Eli reminds her. "It's a bus station."

"Well, maybe that guy over there," I add, indicating a ragged man seated against the wall in a huge carton, padded with assorted grimy blankets and pillows.

Amber emits a little gasp. "He's homeless! I read about that in *USA Today*." She starts toward him.

Tori pulls her back by her ponytail. "Where are you going?"

"We have to help him!" she hisses.

"We can't even help ourselves!" Eli counters.

"People looking out for one another," she lectures, "is the definition of community—"

I cut her off. "If you still believe all that Happy Valley brainwashing, you should have stayed there. Look around—do you see any honesty, harmony, and contentment? This is real life. It's where we come from that's fake."

The thing about Laska is she never backs down. "Just because Serenity turned out to be evil doesn't mean the ideas we learned there were all bad."

Where do I even start? "The question isn't whether Serenity's a good place or a bad place. It's an *un*-place, and the lives we lived there weren't real. We can't judge *here* based on *there*, because *there* was all fake."

Case in point: We're having this conversation while standing stock-still in the middle of the bus station, with people trying to get around us, over us, under us, and through us.

"Out of my way, kids. I've got a bus to catch!"

"Lousy tourists!"

"You got legs inside those jeans?"

"Sorry," I mutter, and drag the others out of the way.

We exit the depot not so much by walking as by allowing ourselves to stumble along with the current of the crowd.

Outside, there's more room, but also more chaos to fill it. The sidewalks are teeming with pedestrians. Vehicles whiz by on the streets. Skyscrapers soar all around us. What do you look at first? Faces? Cars? Signs? Stores? The sounds provide as much variety as the sights—sirens, honking horns, squealing brakes, blaring stereos, leaf blowers, jackhammers, excited shouts. It's like a guy who's been fed bread and water his whole life suddenly stumbling into a humongous feast with every kind of food and drink imaginable.

I'm a clone; my whole life up to now has been a big lie; the people I considered my parents are scientists; I'm on the run from purple commandos; my chances of having any kind of future seem uncertain and very slim—I get all that. But I take a moment to drink it in. A city. A *real* city.

I've spent thirteen years longing for this kind of place. Dreaming about it. And finally, here I am.

We get bumped around a lot because we're staring up at tall buildings instead of walking. There are muttered comments about "stupid kids" and "tourists," which makes no sense, because this is definitely *not* a vacation. Tori is nearly flattened by a little old lady who looks like somebody's grandmother. I take a briefcase in the side from a passing businessman.

I'm not Tori; I ram my shoulder into his chest. Then I stand there defiantly, waiting for him to give me a hard time about it.

He doesn't. He just takes his lumps and keeps on going. Maybe this is how you get along here—by standing up for your space.

"Everybody's so *mean*," Tori complains.

"I don't think they are," Eli muses. "They're just busy. They've got places they have to go and things they need to do."

He's right. People are running for buses, getting into cars and taxis, rushing in and out of stores and office buildings. At least half of them seem to be late, and moving with urgent purpose. Nobody rushes like that in Happy Valley, where anyplace you have to get to is no more than a few minutes away and the last traffic jam was never.

"In Serenity, it only *seemed* like people had busy lives," Amber observes. "Their only real job was watching us."

"Am I supposed to be flattered?" I rumble.

"Let's get off the main street," Eli suggests.

We round the first corner, and turn again down a narrow lane that cuts behind the bus station. At last, quiet—and a chance to stand still without being buffeted from all sides. It's not quite like being back in Serenity, of course. There's a buzz to Denver that never completely goes away. The only buzz in Happy Valley is from the bugs.

It takes us a minute to realize that we're not alone in the alley. About thirty feet away are two guys, and at first, I can't quite figure out what they're doing. For starters, they're a mismatched pair—one guy well dressed and groomed, the other scruffy and unshaven.

Then I catch sight of a glint of metal—a *knife*!

Scruffy has the suit guy up against the wall and is holding the knife to his back.

My heart starts pounding so hard that it echoes in my ears. It's terrifying, and yet I've never been so excited in my life. This is a robbery, a real-life crime!

"Hey!" Suddenly, Amber is running toward the two men. "You stop that!"

Scruffy wheels and now the knife is pointing at Amber.

Eli and Tori are frozen with horror. I have to admit I'm pretty freaked out myself. But Amber is ready to take on the world.

Scruffy takes a threatening step toward her. "Back off, little girl!"

"You back off!" she spits at him.

Believe it or not, the first sign of fear comes from the criminal. "You think I won't cut you because you're a kid?" His voice comes out a little high.

Amber doesn't seem frightened at all. She starts lecturing the crook in what sounds eerily like her mother's teacher voice. "You don't even know who you're robbing. This is a crime against yourself!"

We're all pretty scared, especially the victim, who's

pressed up to the wall, unsure if his mugging is still on.

Scruffy's eyes widen even farther. "Now you're telling me my *business*?"

"Without honesty and harmony," Amber demands, "what chance will you ever have at contentment?"

If the situation wasn't so dangerous, I'd laugh out loud. Leave it to Laska to spout classic Happy Valley garbage to a criminal with a knife!

"Amber . . . ," Eli croaks warningly.

The blade swings in his direction and he clams up. Then Scruffy wields his weapon at his intended victim, who has been inching away from the wall. Finally, he spins to threaten Amber. She doesn't move a muscle, ramrod straight in her fury.

"You're nuts," the crook tells her, and runs out of the alley, disappearing from view.

The rest of us are still quaking in our shoes, too cowed to speak.

"He did the right thing," Amber approves, her anger lifting.

"Maybe *he* did," says the victim, dusting himself off. "Did *you*?"

"I couldn't let him *rob* you," she retorts. "What would you have done if nobody stood up for you?"

"I would have done *this*." He makes an elaborate show of handing her his watch, his wallet, his cell phone, and a gold pinkie ring.

Laska stares at the stash in her open palms. "But you'd lose everything!"

He shakes his head vigorously. "Not everything. I'd still have my life, so I could go out and buy new things. But you—you could have gotten yourself killed! A young kid with everything still ahead of you! Didn't your mother ever teach you not to stick your neck out?"

We gawk at the guy—not just Amber, but all of us. If there was ever a conversation Happy Valley didn't prepare us for, it's this one.

He looks us over, and I can tell he sees how clueless we are. "Let me guess—you kids aren't from around here."

I shuffle uncomfortably. "Not really."

"Where are your parents?"

"We're meeting up with them later," Tori supplies.

The guy thinks it over. He isn't satisfied with what we're telling him, but he seems pressed for time. When he takes his stuff back from Amber, he keeps glancing at the watch.

"A word of advice," he says finally. "Denver can be a tough town. So when your folks aren't around, don't stick your noses into other people's business—especially rough business down some alley. Think about what could have happened to both of us."

"But we—helped you," Amber protests feebly.

"And I'm grateful." He reaches into his wallet, and hands her a twenty-dollar-bill. "For your trouble. Don't ever do it again."

We stand in silence for a few seconds as he hurries out of the alley.

"That's it?" I call at his receding back. "That's all your life is worth? Twenty bucks?"

Eli finds his voice at last. "You know, Amber, that guy's right. That was way too risky."

She's stubborn. "It's never wrong to do what's right."

"It is if it gets you stabbed," Tori reasons.

"He wouldn't have done that."

"Maybe he would; maybe he wouldn't," Eli insists. "You can't take that chance. All this proves is that we're like aliens in the outside world. We have to feel our way through every minute of every day, because it'll only take one mistake to sink us. If you got stabbed and wound up in the hospital, it could make the papers. You think Purple People Eaters can't read?"

"And you could have *died*," Tori adds emotionally. "If

we're going to have a chance to have any kind of future, we all have to pull together."

A discordant note sounds in my head, one that extinguishes any exhilaration I might feel at my first glimpse of a real city. "It's a little late for that," I remind everyone. "We've already lost somebody."

Hector. Poor stupid, pain-in-the-butt little Hector, who died during our escape from Happy Valley. When you discover that you've got no family, your friends mean that much more to you. We "all" can't pull together, because there's no "all" without Hector. Even if we manage to beat the odds and carve out a place for ourselves in this world, Hector will still be gone.

Tori pats my shoulder. "We miss him too, Malik."

They probably do, but not as much as me.

"But we're still here," Eli persists. "We have to go on. We have to eat. We need someplace to sleep."

"Clean clothes," adds Tori. "If we look too grubby, we'll attract attention. And I bet we don't smell so hot too. How much money do we have?"

"Twenty bucks more than before, thanks to Laska," I put in sourly.

"Less than three hundred," Eli reports.

They're getting on my nerves. I'm not done mourning Hector yet. But the future has to be faced—a brand-new city, and a lot of brand-new challenges.

And the Purples are out there still looking for us. We can't forget about that either.

4

AMBER LASKA

It's the biggest piece of plate glass I've ever seen—a window that must be a million feet wide by a million feet high. In it, there's a beach. A whole beach made of plastic—plastic sand, plastic water. And plastic people wearing bathing suits, wraps, shorts, flip-flops, hats, and sunglasses. The clothes are the only part that's real—plus the umbrella and the beach ball.

"I don't get it," says Malik. "What's this supposed to be? Why are the people all fake?"

"It must be some kind of art gallery," Tori suggests. She wrinkles her nose, disappointed. "It isn't very good."

"I think it's a store," Eli puts in. "Look—there are price tags on all the clothes. Not the people, though."

"It can't be a store," I tell them. "This building takes

up a whole block." In Serenity, our general store fits in one room, and that includes the lunch counter, our only restaurant.

Well, if it is a store, they can't be doing much business, because there's no way to go in. We stand, staring for a while, until we notice people entering and exiting what looks like a giant glass paddlewheel on its side.

"That's messed up," Malik announces. "I'm not walking into that thing."

I glare at him. "Don't be such a baby." I step into a wedge-shaped compartment and wait for the contraption to move. It doesn't.

"Is it broken?" Eli wonders.

At that moment, a large lady carrying several shopping bags barrels into the wedge opposite mine on the inside, and gives the glass a shove. The "paddlewheel" turns, whacking me on the behind and tossing me into the store. I stagger into a rack of leather handbags, knocking three of them to the floor.

While I'm straightening up after myself, the others find the courage to navigate the strange entrance and join me. The place is like a kind of fantasyland. The ceiling must be forty feet high, and everything is chrome and crystal and gleaming. Aisles of merchandise stretch as far as the eye can see. And that's just the main floor. They have staircases that move, taking people to upper levels, each one probably just as spectacular and jam-packed with products for sale.

"Well"—you can almost see Eli working it out in his mind—"if our store serves less than two hundred people, when you've got a whole city, you need a bigger one to sell that much more stuff."

"That doesn't explain everything," Tori puts in. "This isn't just more. It's beautiful. Better."

I'm not convinced. "I don't know. How many different kinds of coffeepots do you need? All you want is something to make coffee."

"It's about choice," Tori explains, peering up at the mezzanine at rack after rack of colorful dresses. "That's something we never had."

"It's pointless," I insist. "The outside world has problems—crime, poverty, homelessness. What's more important? Solving them or making lots of junk to sell in gigantic stores?"

The most stunning young woman I've ever seen comes up to Tori and me and shoots a cloud of strong perfume over us.

I start to choke. "What was that for?"

"Melody," she says silkily. "A new fragrance by Bertrand

St. Rene." She drifts off to spray some other poor, unsuspecting soul.

"Man, you guys stink," Malik observes.

"Let's get out of here," Eli decides. "We've got no use for perfume and coffeepots. The things we need are way more basic than that. Food. Shelter."

"And money," adds Malik, checking the price tag on a stainless steel microwave oven. "I think the outside world is expensive."

We manage to catapult ourselves back out through the paddlewheel door. The strong odor of Melody comes with us.

"Okay," says Tori. "Food and shelter."

"Especially food," Malik adds.

They're wrong. If I were making one of my to-do lists for Denver, food, shelter, and money would be on it, sure. But those things wouldn't be at the top.

THINGS TO DO TODAY (ABSOLUTELY PRIORITIZED)

- Figure out where we stand . . .

We're clones—exact genetic copies of some seriously bad criminals. We have no parents. We were created in test tubes using cells of the people we're cloned from. Fine, we get that. It's kind of gross, and a little mind-blowing, but there's no point in obsessing over it, because here we are. The one thing we can't do is change the past.

The real question is how do clones fit into society? Are there a lot of us? I can't stop scanning the vast crowds of people in downtown Denver. How many of them are clones? One percent? Ten percent? More? Could it be a common thing? Randy didn't think so.

And how do you tell who's who? The McNally students didn't seem any different from us, and neither did the non-Osiris Serenity kids.

So what's our status? Are clones the same as regular people? Are we second-class citizens? Outcasts? Monsters, even? And what about the criminals we're cloned from? Do we get blamed for their bad deeds? Are we criminals, too, because of them? That seems pretty unfair, but anything is possible. The truth is we don't know. We might as well have just landed on another planet.

"First things first," I tell the others. "We need to find out what it means to be a clone."

"I wish I had my iPad," Eli says wistfully. "We need the internet."

We had internet in Serenity, but it turned out to be fake. Project Osiris controlled everything we were exposed to.

We wander around awhile, peering into shop windows with wide eyes. It seems crazy that you can buy toilet paper in one store and then walk next door where they'll sell you a five-thousand-dollar handbag. Not far down the block is a huge display of movies. We recognize a few, but anything with guns or explosions or fighting on the cover is completely new to us.

Tori points across the street. "How about that place? They have internet."

I read the sign:

BITES AND BYTES
INTERNET CAFÉ AND THINK TANK
TRY OUR WORLD-FAMOUS HOMEMADE HUMMUS

"They have *food*," Malik amends. "Let's go."

"We have to be careful with our money," Eli reminds us.

"You'll save a fortune in funeral expenses when I don't starve to death," Malik assures him.

I won't try to say Bites and Bytes is a nice place or even a bad one, because we have absolutely nothing to compare it to. This place smells like coffee, but it's pretty clean, with computers on all the tables.

The other customers look up when we come in. Once

again, I'm expecting someone to yell out a clone warning and tackle us while the cashier pulls the clone alarm. Then the police will send the clone squad to put us in clone-cuffs and haul us away to clone prison.

I've got to get a grip.

The customers go back to their snacking and web surfing, and we find a free table. Eli slides in behind the keyboard, and the rest of us head up to the counter.

Note to self: Never buy food when you're super hungry. We clean that place out, spending far more than any of us want to admit to Eli. We even try the world-famous home-made hummus. Within minutes, every last crumb is gone.

There's something about watching Eli when he's on the internet. His fingers dance across the keyboard at improbable speeds, and his concentration is so perfect that you could shoot off fireworks next to his ear and he wouldn't notice.

The web pages pile up, overlaying one another on the screen: definitions of *clone*; history of cloning; medical details; cloning technology; "To Clone or Not to Clone; An Ethical Analysis"; cloning and animals . . .

"Don't keep us in suspense," Malik prods. "Are we human or what?"

"How many others are there just like us?" I add.

At last, Eli leans back. "None," he replies. We can barely hear him.

"None?" Tori echoes.

"Scientists have experimented with cloning cells," Eli explains faintly. "They've cloned animals, with different degrees of success. No people."

"You mean we're *it*?" demands Malik.

"According to this," Eli explains, "the larger and more complex the organism, the harder it is to clone. But the main reason there are no human clones is"—he takes a deep breath—"human cloning is illegal in every single country in the world."

We're silent as this sinks in. Over the past weeks we've come to accept the fact that we're clones. But never did we consider that we might be the only ones.

Tori finds her shaky voice first. "I always knew Project Osiris was kind of mad science-y. But this makes us . . . freaks."

Eli and Malik are pale as ghosts.

"Are you kidding?" I crow. "This is the best news I've heard since we busted out of Serenity!"

Malik glares at me. "How do you figure that?"

"Think!" I insist. "This is proof positive that the whole Project Osiris is a *crime*! Don't you see? All we have to do is go to the police and tell them about it. And if they ask for evidence, it's *us*."

"I don't know if that's such a good idea," Eli says. "I mean, we were nervous about revealing ourselves as clones when we thought there were probably others. But now we'll be telling them that a whole new type of human exists. That's going to be a big shock."

"All the more reason why they can't ignore us," I argue.

"And when the cops ask us who we're clones of?" Malik prompts.

"We'll tell the truth," I reply readily. "That isn't our fault either. None of us are crooks; we're just cloned from them. The real criminals in all this are our so-called parents. When we expose Osiris, the police will arrest them and shut down Serenity for the fraud that it is."

"I'm not so sure I want my parents arrested," Tori says unsteadily. "Maybe they deserve it, but . . ." Her voice trails off.

Malik's face is flushed and even Eli looks a little torn. His "dad," Felix Hammerstrom, is the top dog of Project Osiris. If anybody needs to be locked up, it's him. Believe me, I understand. When I picture my "mother," I don't see evil; I see Mom. We weren't mistreated or abused. We felt loved. Maybe we *were* loved in a way. But that doesn't change the fact that the reason our families resembled real families is it was part of the *experiment.*

"Listen, you guys," I tell them, "I know it's tough to turn on the people who raised you. It's tough for me too. But when the Purples came after us at McNally, who do you think sent them? We'll never be free until we take down Project Osiris once and for all."

They don't look convinced, which, frankly, amazes me. It's a big decision, but it isn't a very hard one. Right is right, and wrong is wrong. What more than that do they need?

I play my trump card. "It isn't just about us, you know. There are six more kids just like us still in Serenity under Osiris's thumb. We owe them the same chance at a life that we want for ourselves."

"Good point," Eli concedes. "They're all good points. But we have to be careful to think everything through before we do anything rash."

"For how long?" I shoot back. "Until the Purples catch up with us and drag us back to Serenity?" I glance out the café window and immediately spot a uniformed police officer. He's standing in the middle of a busy intersection, directing the traffic with hand signals and a whistle. "Trust me."

"Amber, wait—" Tori pleads.

But I'm already running out the front door. There's no time like the present for doing the right thing. I learned that from Mom in Contentment class. I take some satisfaction in using a Serenity slogan to help put an end to their sick game.

The instant I step into the road, there's angry honking, screeching brakes, and I'm almost hit by a taxi. In the outside world, even when you're doing the right thing, you'd better watch where you're going. By the time I make it to the policeman, I must be wild-eyed and breathless.

He's not pleased with me. "What's your problem, kid? Haven't you ever seen a red light before?"

Well, not before a few days ago. But it's more important to get to the point. "I want to report a crime!"

His eyes are suddenly alert. "What crime?"

"Human cloning."

He looks startled. "That's a new one on me. We don't get much human cloning in the traffic department."

I have to shout to be heard over the engine noise and honking. "I'm part of an experiment in Serenity, New Mexico. They made eleven clones, but only four of us escaped—"

He cuts me off. "You know, interfering with a police officer in the performance of his duty is against the law. Do you think this is some kind of joke? People are trying to get places. And they can't, because you're out here pulling my chain."

"I'm trying to tell you about a serious crime—an experiment called Project Osiris!"

"Where's your mother?" he demands.

"Aren't you listening?" I explode. "I don't have a mother! I'm a clone!"

I guess I finally get through to him, because his anger and impatience disappear. He starts the traffic moving again, and speaks into his walkie-talkie. "I need a black-and-white. I've got a situation here."

We make our way to the far corner.

"Thank you for listening to me," I say gratefully. "I know this must be a shock. We only learned the truth ourselves a couple of weeks ago."

"Uh-huh."

A police car pulls up to the curb, and I'm bundled into the backseat. I'm filled with a very Serenity-like sense of righteous justice. It won't be easy to watch our parents put on trial, but this is the best course for us—the only course, really. The others will thank me in the end.

The traffic cop speaks to the driver. "Tell them to call a shrink who works with kids."

The rear door locks engage with a loud click.

"No!" I cry. "I'm not crazy! It's the truth!" I yank at the handle but it clicks uselessly.

The black-and-white makes a wide U-turn and heads for the police station. The last thing I see before we roar away is Eli, Tori, and Malik, their faces pressed against the front window of Bites and Bytes.

They don't look grateful. They look very, very scared.

5

TORI PRITEL

The sight of that police car driving away with Amber is one of the most awful things I've ever seen. (And I've seen a lot of awful things lately.)

Malik is pacing on the sidewalk in front of Bites and Bytes. "We begged her not to do anything stupid! And what does she do? Something stupid!"

"You can't blame her," I defend my best friend. "None of us understand how things work in the outside world."

"Which is why it makes sense to do *nothing*!" Malik insists. "But that's not good enough for Laska! She knows better!"

Eli takes off down the block in a futile attempt to keep up with the car. His desperation triggers the same response in Malik and me. If we lose track of Amber in this huge city, we'll never lay eyes on her again.

It's all my fault. Amber's my best friend. I should have been keeping an eye on her. She took the news about Project Osiris harder than any of us. Why didn't I know that if she believed she had an easy fix for our situation, she'd jump into it without thinking?

We can still see the squad car, but it gets harder to spot as it pulls away, and traffic fills in the street behind it. To make matters worse, the sidewalks are crowded, and we're scrambling around an obstacle course of pedestrians and dogs and mailboxes and fire hydrants. Malik gets stuck behind two guys carrying a couch and loses ground. I avoid them, dance around a garbage can, and catch up to Eli.

"We lost her!" he pants.

Not me. I've trained myself to notice details other people miss (back when I thought my future would be as an artist, not a fugitive). The police car is distant, but I've got it in my sights—it's sandwiched between an SUV and a city bus. Lacking the breath for a verbal answer, I point.

We're just about to blast through the next intersection when a big semi lumbers right out in front of us. Eli and I practically run into it, but manage to pull up mere inches from the trailer's vast paneled side. We have no choice. We stand flat-footed, waiting for it to inch into the main road.

Malik catches up to us, shaking his fist at the driver. "You got a gas pedal on that thing?"

The driver yells back a word I've never heard before, although I'm pretty sure it's rude. (Malik might fit perfectly into the outside world.)

And then the truck moves on, opening up our view of the road ahead. The police car is obviously gone, and Amber with it.

I'm running again. "Hurry!" I call back. "We can't lose her."

Eli shakes his head sadly. "We already have. That car could have turned down any one of these side streets."

"She's history," Malik confirms.

I'm normally pretty levelheaded, but this is too much. "You mean that's *it*? Bye-bye Amber, nice knowing you?"

"We can maybe hang around Bites and Bytes," Eli suggests lamely. "On the off-chance she gets loose, maybe it'll occur to her to look for us there."

"How's she going to get loose?" I demand. "She isn't lost; she's under arrest! The Purples are obviously in touch with the Denver Police, and they're going to hear that a thirteen-year-old girl got picked up by the cops in District Six! They'll scoop her up so fast, she'll be back in Serenity by nightfall."

"District Six?" Malik repeats. "Where'd you get that?"

I'm upset. "It was printed on the door of the squad car! If you stopped stuffing your face long enough to open your eyes, you might see something!"

"District Six," Eli repeats, and you can almost see the wheels turning inside his logical mind. "The city must be carved up into police districts!"

I struggle to contain my surge of hope. We haven't found Amber—not yet.

But at least we have something to go on.

Back at Bites and Bytes, it takes Eli just a few seconds to find the website of the Denver Police Department. Turns out, we're right about the districts. Better yet, each district has its own separate police station.

"Where they take pinheads who get themselves arrested!" Malik exclaims.

"Here's the address of the District Six precinct house." Deftly, Eli copies the information, calls up a map program, and pastes the details into the search field. According to the computer, it's only 0.9 miles away, on North Washington.

"So now what?" Malik challenges as we head over there. "We can't exactly knock on the door of the station and say 'Give us back our dimwit.'"

"We'll just have to wing it," Eli decides. "We don't even know how much trouble she's in. Maybe they'll just ask her a few questions and cut her loose."

"Maybe," I agree. (But deep down, I'm thinking: *We couldn't get that lucky.*)

We know we're in the right place even before we see the police station itself. There are squad cars parked on both sides of the block, and officers coming and going everywhere. We're from Serenity, where the only uniforms are worn by Purples. So we're already on edge by the time we reach the door.

For some reason, I'm struck by a random flashback—dress-up party, my fifth birthday, or maybe even my fourth. I'm Ariel from *The Little Mermaid*, fishtail and all. I forget which of the princesses Amber's dressed as.

And now we have to spring her from the police. How times have changed.

Malik swallows hard. "Who knows what Laska told the cops about us? We could get arrested too."

I nod. "Good point. Only one of us should go in. That leaves two more on the outside just in case we need to do a double rescue."

"I'll go," Eli volunteers. "What do I say?"

I mull it over. "If Amber told them anything about

Serenity, Purple People Eaters, or clones, they might think she's crazy. So say she's your sister. You brought her into the city for a psychiatrist's appointment and she took off on you. It's a big mess—you're looking everywhere, your parents are worried sick, and if you don't get to the doctor's right away, you'll miss the appointment. Make up a name. Dr. Reiner. His office is on Main Street—I'm pretty sure every big city has a Main Street. Got it?"

They both stare at me.

"What?" I ask.

"I don't know about harmony and contentment," Malik says with respect, "but it didn't take you very long to unlearn honesty."

"You're kind of good at this," Eli agrees.

"There's obviously nothing to be good at," I tell them. "You just think about the result you want and the result you don't want, and figure out a story that'll get you the good thing and avoid the bad one."

"You should do it," Malik concludes. "You're the best liar."

In Serenity, we were always taught that nothing is worse than being dishonest. "It's not lying. It's strategy."

"Don't take it personally," he shoots back. "It's not your fault you got cloned from some crook who wouldn't know the truth if she tripped over it. Look at the bright side. At least she's not a murderer."

"You'd better hope," I seethe.

That's how I end up being the one who marches into the police station to try to talk Amber out of custody. (I suppose it's only fair—she's *my* best friend.)

I don't know what I expect—rows of cells, prisoners staring out through the bars, and one of them Amber. But inside I find a dreary waiting room with a desk sergeant at the front.

My first thought is: *Who decorated this place?* In Serenity, everything is brand-new and really nice: tasteful colors, rich fabrics, stylish furniture. This looks like the place old desks go to die. Everything is beige, and you can tell most of it didn't start out that way.

I march right up to the sergeant. She ignores me, so I clear my throat. "Excuse me, I think my sister was brought here."

She looks interested. "Your sister got a name?"

I hesitate. Amber might have given them a fake name, but I doubt it. Her whole purpose was to bring the law down on Project Osiris. She said it herself: *we're* the evidence.

I chance it. "Amber Laska. I'm her sister, Victoria."

Malik might be right about me and lying. It's kind of scary how totally easily the whoppers trip off my tongue as I launch into my story about the psychiatrist's appointment, and how "Dad" drove us in from Pueblo just that morning.

The sergeant leans back in her chair. "Don't suppose you've got any ID? Student card? Bus pass?"

"Uh—no." The question throws me a little. I've never had any identification—none of us have. What's the point of ID in a town where everybody knows everybody else?

"How come it's you who came for your sister instead of your folks?"

"So she's here?" I probe.

She nods. "Squad car brought her in half an hour ago. I can't release her, though."

"Is she under arrest?"

"No, but she's a minor and so are you. Your parents will have to come get her."

That would be a neat trick. "I don't know where they are," I plead, inventing rapidly. "Everyone panicked when Amber disappeared. We split up to look for her."

The sergeant hands me her cell phone. "Call them."

With the officer watching me, I have to punch in

numbers, but I never place the call. "Nobody's picking up." I "try" again, without pressing dial. "Mom, if you get this message, I found Amber. She's at the police station on North Washington, but they won't let me take her. You have to come right away or we'll miss the appointment, and who knows when they'll have another one . . ." By this time, I'm actually crying, and it isn't part of the act. How are we going to get Amber out of this place? We can't produce parents out of thin air.

"Kid—" the desk sergeant tries to soothe.

"Aurora," I blubber aloud.

She frowns. "Thought your name's Victoria."

"Princess Aurora—from *Sleeping Beauty*. That's who Amber was at my dress-up party." It occurs to me how ridiculous this must seem. "Forget it. It was a long time ago . . ."

The desk sergeant looks a little alarmed at the prospect of having two crazy sisters to deal with instead of just one. "I see you're upset and I want to help if I can. We're taking your sister to see our psychologist at five o'clock. This is his office." She scribbles a name and address on the back of a business card and hands it to me. "Maybe your folks can meet you there. If you have any trouble finding them, you come straight back here, you hear me?"

"Thanks," I say, and I'm honestly grateful. I don't have Amber, but I have the next best thing.

We know where she's going to be and when.

Now we have to go get her.

6

ELI FRIEDEN

A few months ago, this would have been science fiction. We were living in Serenity, 100 percent convinced it was the best place on earth. Even Malik, who complained about how boring it was, was just blustering when he talked about leaving one day. What little we knew about the outside world centered around the fact that we didn't want to go there—it was lawless; it was dirty; it was horrible.

Now we're right smack dab in the middle of that world, and most of the lawless, dirty, and horrible things we've seen here are being done by *us*. And don't think it doesn't haunt us that this makes perfect sense. After all, we're supposed to be exact copies of some of the worst criminals the human race has to offer.

Haunting or not, though, we don't have time to worry

that we might be living up to the evil in our DNA. We have to get Amber back. Period.

Finding the Medical Arts Center isn't so easy. Everyone we ask assures us it's not far, and then launches into a long, complicated series of twists and turns, complete with instructions like "at the third light," and "there's a shoemaker on the corner." Hey, we come from a town where there are no traffic lights, and the shoes we wear are made someplace else.

Eventually, we start to get nervous, because Amber's appointment is at five. If we miss her there, we might never catch up with her again. The smart move would be to go back to Bites and Bytes and look up the address on a computer. But by this point, we're so turned around that we can't figure out where that is either. We're just about in a panic, when Tori stumbles on a kiosk that gives away tourist maps of downtown.

A few frenzied minutes later, we run up to the Medical Arts Center on Delaware Street, which we must have passed and ignored at least five times. I guess that's to be expected when you're used to a place where the total number of roads falls in the single digits.

It's a four-story brick building with a flat roof, not as old and run down as the police station, but nowhere near as new and nice as anything in Serenity.

"Why does everything in the outside world have to be so blah?" Tori wonders.

"I have a theory about that," I tell her. "Serenity wasn't a real town, so they could concentrate on making it look good. But out here, everything serves a real purpose. A medical building doesn't have to be an architectural masterpiece. It just has to be a place where you can see your doctor."

Malik snorts impatiently. "We'll ask them to put up streamers and balloons for our next kidnapping."

The building is nicer on the inside, but not much, with painted cinderblock walls and fluorescent lighting. It's clean, though, and the elevator works. None of us have ever been in an elevator before, and we're a little embarrassed by how excited we get by it. We even go up to the fourth floor so we can come down to the third. It's a pretty big deal. Malik and Tori have a little argument over who pushes the button.

The third floor features a long hallway, each door leading to a different medical practice. There are several doctors, a dentist, a chiropractor, and something called an aromatherapist, whatever that is. But our center of focus is the office marked:

306
DR. EMIL HERZOG
GENERAL PSYCHIATRY

"So what do we do?" asks Malik. "Hide in one of these doorways, and when we see Laska, grab her and run down the stairs?"

I shake my head. "That won't work. They're not going to send her by herself. She'll be with a cop."

Tori scans the third floor with an appraiser's eye. She walks to the ladies' room, a few doors past 306, peers inside, and motions us to join her.

"We can't go in there," I hiss. "It's for girls."

Malik favors me with a smile. "If you're too chicken to set foot inside the girls' bathroom, I kind of doubt you're ready to jack a prisoner from police custody."

He has a point. We're done with the sweetness and good manners we learned in Serenity. It's a jungle out here. If you can't climb up the food chain, something's going to eat you.

Tori opens the bathroom door and makes us go inside. There are four stalls and two sinks, but she immediately moves to the large window at the far end. We join her and peer down into a shaded alley at the back of the building.

"We're on the third floor," I remind her. "How do we get down?"

"We could buy a rope," Malik suggests. "There must be a hardware store around here somewhere."

Tori consults her watch. "No time. It's quarter to five. How high up do you think this is?"

"High enough to break our legs and probably our necks too," puts in Malik.

"There must be something here we can use to climb down . . . ," Tori muses.

We follow her back out of the bathroom. She walks briskly down the hall looking from side to side.

Malik is impatient. "It's a building full of doctors. What are we going to do—make a ladder out of tongue depressors?"

She stops in front of a large glass case built into the wall. Inside, wrapped up in a tight coil, is the third-floor fire hose.

I'm standing in the Medical Arts Center's glass lobby when the squad car pulls up to the curb. The sign says *No Parking*, but that doesn't seem to apply to police. A big cop opens the rear door and Amber gets out. My heart soars at the sight of her familiar face.

As they start up the walk, I slip out the front door and move toward them. The instant Amber spots me, I shake my head no. She can't acknowledge me, or the cop will get suspicious.

I jostle her arm as I pass by. "Excuse me."

"Watch where you're going, kid," the cop growls.

"Sorry," I apologize, and manage to whisper into Amber's ear, *"Third-floor bathroom."*

I'm scared to death that the cop heard me—or that Amber didn't. But I won't know that until she shows up in the ladies' room. Or doesn't.

I dart around and reenter the building from the parking lot door. From there, I fly up the stairs and hit the third floor just as the elevator doors rumble open behind me. I turn on the jets and blast into the bathroom, where Malik and Tori are waiting anxiously.

"She's here?" Tori asks.

I nod, panting. "With the biggest cop you've ever seen. Considering she's not under arrest, they're sure treating her like a prisoner."

Malik and I hide in two stalls, standing on the toilet seats so our feet won't show. If somebody else needs to use the bathroom before Amber gets here, the last thing we need is some lady screaming the third floor down.

Five minutes pass. Then ten.

Tori's getting antsy. "Maybe they won't let her go."

"They have to let her go." But what if she didn't receive my whispered message in the first place?

Before I can express this to the others, I hear the door opening. A deep voice rumbles, "I'll wait outside."

When Malik and I exit the stalls, we find a very silent hugging reunion in progress between the two girls.

"I'd kill you if I wasn't so glad to see you," Malik whispers.

Amber reddens. "I screwed up. I should have known that they wouldn't believe me."

Tori is all business. "We can blame each other later. Let's get out of here."

"How?" rasps Amber. "That cop's right outside."

Tori reaches under the closest stall and pulls out the fire hose. One end has been firmly knotted to base of the metal divider. "Help me with the window."

Malik flips the latch and lifts. The sash doesn't budge.

I move in to give him a hand. We heave with all our might. Nothing.

Amber examines the frame. "It's painted shut."

"We'll smash the window," Malik offers.

"No!" Amber hisses. "That cop will hear it."

Tori pulls a barrette out of her hair and begins to break through the thick layer of dried paint with the metal clip. It works, but it's slow going.

There's a rap at the bathroom door. "What's taking so long in there?"

"You want details?" Amber shoots back.

The knocking stops.

Sweat forms on Tori's brow as she uses the barrette to saw all the way around the frame. At last, she steps back and Malik and I try again. The window resists for a moment and then rises in a shower of paint chips.

Tori tosses the nozzle out the window and we watch the hose unroll down the side of the building. But instead of dropping all the way to the alley, the length plays out and the nozzle hangs there, ten feet off the ground.

"We're short," I report.

The others peer outside at our dangling mode of escape.

Malik is furious. "Didn't you bother to make sure the rope was long enough?" He looks like he's shouting, but it comes out an agitated snarl.

"We'll have to climb down as far as we can and jump the rest of the way," Tori decides.

"I don't know," I say nervously. "With a drop like that, at least one of us is bound to sprain an ankle or worse. If that cop chases us, we'll be dead meat."

"If we don't get out of here now, we're dead meat anyway," Amber argues.

Tori leans over the sash. "See that Dumpster off to the left? When you get to the bottom of the hose, try to swing toward it. At least it's a soft landing."

"But it's *garbage*," Malik complains.

We all know that his real concern is rappelling down a three-story building, swinging like Tarzan, and then jumping into what we hope is something soft. Yeah, we're all a little worried about that.

The cop is knocking again. "Hurry up, Amber. The doctor's waiting."

My mind forms the connections—the officer, the Purples, my dad. The thought of Felix Frieden is all the motivation I need. "I'll go first." I scramble out the window, clinging to the fabric of the hose.

"Let me just wash up," Amber calls in the direction of the door. I hear one of the toilets flushing.

I don't know what's worse—the climb itself or the fear that the slightest slip will leave me dashed to pieces on the pavement of a Denver alley. The simple act of letting go to lower myself is a stomach-churning terror. To make matters worse, every time I bounce back to the wall, the rough brick rips my knuckles to shreds. When I finally reach the dangling nozzle, it's a shock how far up I still am, and an even bigger shock how far away the Dumpster is.

I turn beseeching eyes up to the third floor.

Tori mouths a single word: "Swing!"

I wriggle my body in an attempt to get the hose in motion.

"Sometime today would be nice," comes from above. Malik.

It's no use. I'm swaying a little but the Dumpster still looks out of range. I'm going to have to leap for it. And if I miss—well, we won't go into that.

I can't do it. Dangling from a fire hose may not be the most comfortable position, but at least I'm attached to something solid. How am I going to work up the courage to let go?

I manufacture an image of Dad, a smug, superior expression on his face, and I'm as ready as I'll ever be.

Jump!

I extend my legs like a trapeze artist and fling myself at the Dumpster. For an instant I'm in midair, uncoupled from earth, falling. Then I'm rolling in the garbage. It's not the softest impact, but it's a lot softer than the pavement. I lurch to a stop with my face in a half-eaten pizza, disturbing a squadron of feasting flies.

There was definitely a moment when I was in free fall, not knowing if I'd survive it, where I'd have traded my situation for a return to Serenity. I'll never admit it to the others, but it was definitely there.

I get up, battered but not broken, to see Tori headed down the hose, moving with an ease and skill that I could never match. In no time at all, she's at the bottom, swinging like a pendulum out over the Dumpster. She lands on her feet beside me. High above, Malik throws a leg out the window and begins his descent. That means Amber will be last, probably because her police escort is getting antsy and needs to hear her voice through the door.

"How's that cop?" I ask.

"Mad." Tori's nervous. "And getting madder. The minute he doesn't hear Amber's voice anymore he's going to barge into the bathroom and see the fire hose going out the window."

"We'll have to run for it. We should have a little head start while he leaves the building. But the minute he gets in his car, the advantage is all his."

Malik is the strongest of us, but he's also carrying the most weight. He's climbing cautiously, his style closer to mine than Tori's.

"Why's he going so slow?" Tori murmurs under her breath.

"Maybe he's afraid of breaking every bone in his body," I tell her. "I know I was."

And then he's crashing into the Dumpster beside us, practically bowling us over, landing flat on his face.

He rolls over in the trash, groaning. "It stinks in here!"

"What do you expect the garbage to smell like?" I retort. "Roses?"

Now Amber is on the way down, moving almost as quickly as Tori, her arms working like pistons. Her expression is wild as she mouths an urgent message without making any sound.

"You're doing fine," Tori calls.

A minute later, the cause of her distress becomes clear. The big cop is leaning out the window. He takes in the sight of Amber on the hose and us in the Dumpster and bellows, "Freeze!"

And when we don't freeze, he does something even Tori hasn't anticipated. He grips ham-like hands on the fire hose and begins yanking Amber up. Panicking, she descends faster. But the cop is strong as an ox, and she actually starts to rise.

"Jump!" yells Tori.

Amber is petrified. "It's too high!"

You'd better believe it's too high, but we can't let her be hauled back into custody.

"We'll catch you," I promise.

Malik casts me a look that plainly says nobody's going to be able to catch anybody. But he's holding out his arms. For Amber, jumping is a bad option, but also the only one there is.

She's at least twenty feet up when she kicks toward us.

The cop stops pulling. "Don't do it, kid!"

It's too late. Amber lets go. It's almost a swan dive. We scramble to guess the point of impact, because she's going to snap her neck if we don't catch her. I have an awful flashback to my last sight of poor Hector, clinging to the back of the cone truck right before it plunged off the road and down into the steep valley.

Please don't let us lose anybody else.

Despite her toughness, Amber is screaming all the way. We all know we'll be crushed like bugs if she lands on us, but *she'll* be crushed if we just let her drop. We reach up, and suddenly she's there, coming down between us. We each get a hand on her before the force of her fall slams the four of us into the refuse of the Dumpster.

"Amber!" Tori is frantic. "Are you okay?"

"I—I think so." Amber sits up in the trash, moving all her limbs, taking stock of herself.

"I'm alive," croaks Malik. "No thanks to Laska."

"Kid?" comes an anxious voice from above. It's the cop, and he's more worried than mad.

It's a good news/bad news kind of thing. It's good that nobody's hurt. But then he disappears, which can only mean one thing.

He's coming after us.

7

MALIK BRUDER

I should kill Amber for putting us through this.

But right now I'm too busy running for my life.

One by one, we climb out of the Dumpster and drop to the pavement. We're covered in coffee grounds and pizza grease, and my nose is bleeding. But under the circumstances, we're lucky.

We dash down the alley to the next street, and find an even narrower alley off of there. We hug the wall, peering out just in time to see the police cruiser pass by on the main road, our cop hunched over the wheel, looking from side to side.

Thanks so much, Laska. We don't have enough trouble with Project Osiris on the hunt for us. We need the law breathing down our necks. If that cop catches us, it won't be just Amber who's in trouble. He'll arrest all four of us this time. I wonder if there's such a crime as aiding and abetting a moron.

"We've got to get out of here," Amber says urgently.

"You think?" I ask sarcastically.

Eli's not so sure. "Maybe it makes more sense to lie low."

Laska shakes her head. "His car has a police radio in it. I heard it while we were driving to the medical building—all these cops telling each other what to watch for. He could have every officer in Denver on the lookout for four kids."

It's not good. If the Purples hear about four runaways, it's not going to take them long to put two and two together. Either they'll find us first, or the cops will, and we'll be sitting ducks in a cell when Serenity's goon squad comes to drag us back to Happy Valley. We can try to explain what's happened. But Laska's already proven how believable our clone story is out here in the real world.

"We could separate, and meet back when the heat's off," Tori suggests.

"No way!" I exclaim. "Two stupids don't make a smart. We almost got ourselves killed getting Laska back. We're not going to break up on purpose."

"We need to stick together," Eli agrees. "But we also need

to be miles away from where they're going to be searching for us. How do people get around a city?"

"We had the Purples' car," I remind him, "but that wasn't good enough for you."

"We had to ditch it," Eli defends the decision. "The Purples were following us by air."

"People take buses," Tori reasons, "and trains—"

"Those things are full of passengers," Eli cuts in. "Someone is bound to remember four kids and where they got off."

"What about a taxi?" Amber suggests.

"Even worse," Eli replies seriously. "The driver could be listening to the radio and hear about the search. At best he'd know exactly where he dropped us. At worst, we could be still in the car when it happens."

"Well, what are we supposed to do?" I ask belligerently. "Flap our arms and fly?"

While we stand there, looking helplessly at each other, a police car cruises by on the street at the opposite end of our alley. I can tell we're all wondering the same thing—is that the same cop, or has he sounded the alarm, and we're already being surrounded?

"What we need," Tori muses, "is a ride from someone who doesn't know he's giving us a ride."

"Oh, right!" I explode. "Like there's somebody that blind or that stupid!"

We hear a loud grinding sound as a truck gears down to come to a halt. For a moment, it fills the opening at the end of the lane before stopping just past it. The driver jumps out, and disappears into a small luncheonette.

Suddenly, as if drawn by some invisible magnet, Tori is scampering toward it.

"What are you doing?" I hiss. One girl trying to get me killed per day is my limit.

Urgently, she motions us over to join her. It's a medium-size dump truck with a cherry-picker attachment on the back. The sign on the cab door reads: *McHenry's Tree Service, LLC.* The bed is overflowing with leafy branches and twigs.

"So what?" I challenge in a whisper.

"Don't you get it?" Tori insists. "In Serenity, that company from Taos used to come to trim the branches away from roofs and power lines. Did they dump the cuttings in the center of town? No. They took them somewhere else." She regards us meaningfully. "We want to go somewhere else."

"You mean we stow away in there?" Eli asks.

My jaw must be stuck out at least three inches. "I refuse."

"What's the matter?" Amber challenges. "Are you afraid of a few sticks?"

"Not the sticks." My face feels hot. "The bugs."

She's thunderstruck. "Wait—you're afraid of bugs? *You?*"

"Not *afraid.* I just don't like them. The Dumpster was bad enough with those flies. Who knows what's living in all these trees!"

"Listen, Malik," Eli begins. "We're all doing stuff we don't like—"

A police siren cuts the air. I scramble up the side of that truck so fast I probably leave a smoke trail. I vault over the edge of the bed and disappear into the leafy branches. I hear the rustling and snapping of the others piling in beside me.

As I burrow lower into the dense green cuttings, twigs scratch at my face and arms. There are thicker branches too, and I roll onto one, nearly skewering myself, shish-kebab style. My head collides with something hard.

"Ow!" Amber's voice.

I hope it hurts.

"Is everybody here?" Tori asks.

"Do you mean us, or the caterpillars?" I reply. They're everywhere—worms with fur coats. The garbage was miserable, but at least it wasn't *alive*. My skin is crawling.

The sirens are all around us now; no one is disputing whether or not we did the right thing. We lie low, not that we have a lot of choice. It feels like forever, but it's probably only ten more minutes.

The door of the cab slams, and the truck starts up again. And then we're away. Every motion of the heavy vehicle inflicts more bruises, more scratches, and more itchy discomfort. It's stop and start for a while, and then we accelerate to a steady speed.

"I think we're on a highway," Amber calls.

With great effort, I crawl/swim/climb to the "surface" and peer over the side of the truck. Tori guessed right. The tall buildings of Denver's core are behind us; we're leaving town, not exactly safe, but at least we're putting some distance between ourselves and the police search.

I burrow back down and report to the others.

"How do we know when to get off?" Amber asks.

"That's easy," says Tori. "When we stop."

"Let's hope this isn't an express to Massachusetts," I grumble.

Tori laughs. "I don't know much about Massachusetts, but I'm pretty sure they've got their own branches. They don't need to truck them in from Colorado."

It's an uncomfortable ride, but no one is complaining, not even me. The farther we get from downtown Denver, the greater our sense of hope that we might have avoided the disaster that very nearly put an end to our brief shot at freedom.

After several more minutes, the truck slows, and we can tell we're off the highway.

"Get ready," Tori advises. "The next time we stop, we should make a run for it."

The McHenry's truck makes several turns, but never actually halts. At last, we feel the momentary sense of braking, and emerge from our hiding place, ready to leap for it. All at once, we're backing up, our vehicle emitting a series of warning beeps.

"What's going on?" demands Amber.

Finally, we stop. That is to say, the truck does. The bed is tilting, so we are too. Behind us—quickly becoming below us—a loud electric grinding begins, the kind of noise where you feel the vibration in your teeth below the gum line. Eventually, the bed rises so high that the contents—and that includes us—begin to slide. The back flap lifts on a hydraulic motor, and the branches start to pour out. The grinding becomes a whole lot louder, and a cloud of dust is thrown back at us, stinging our eyes and making breathing difficult. Through it, we can see a huge metal hopper and, inside it, the whirling cutting blades of a wood chipper.

"Get out! Get out! *Now!*" I scream.

We try to move in the opposite direction, but it's like trying to run straight up. We're part of the load, and the load is being drawn inexorably into the maw of the machine.

I crawl to the side of the truck bed, and clamp both arms over the top. Eli tries to do the same, but the slope is pulling him down too quickly.

I throw out a leg, accidentally kicking him in the stomach. "Grab hold!"

He latches onto my foot, locking it into his armpit. Tori comes up behind me and throws her arms around my neck. That's three of us accounted for. Where's Laska?

I spot her. She's clenching a thick branch sliding down the center of the payload, screaming in terror. In desperation, Eli reaches out for her with his free hand. He misses Amber, but gets just enough of the branch to stop its descent. God only knows how he stays attached to me and still hangs onto the branch and Amber. But the bed is close to full vertical at this point, and the choice has become starkly simple: we hold on, or we get sliced and diced.

I'm yelling my head off in agony and exertion. My grip on the side of the truck is what's keeping everybody from falling. Amber's howling, Tori's weeping. You can barely hear any of it over the shriek of the cutting blades.

I don't know how it happens. One minute, I'm clamped to the side; the next, I'm not. We're skidding along the dumper, still attached to one another, but heading down toward the lethal blades. We're going to die and all I can think is it's my fault.

In the noise and chaos, we never hear the hydraulic motor that closes the truck's back flap. The next thing I know, Amber yelps in pain, as the three of us fall on top of her, crushing her against the metal barrier that has just saved our lives.

The bed is coming down again, lowering to horizontal. My heartbeat, though, is anything but normal. We were so close to being dead. If the back flap had stayed open a split second longer . . .

We're clones who came from nothing and no one, and we would have been gone as if we'd never existed.

Somehow, we manage to climb over the side and jump to the ground and roll. When I try to get up again, my legs have turned to rubber.

Eli is the first to make it to his feet. "Move!" he hisses. "Before we get run over by our own escape truck!"

We manage to get up and stagger clear. That's when the

driver of the truck spots us for the first time.

"Hey, what are you kids doing here? This is a restricted area!"

"Sorry," Tori calls, during a pretty good job of sounding off-hand, considering what we've just been through. "We were looking for a place to play soccer."

"What—here? One of these machines could take your arm off and chop it into hamburger!"

"Yeah, right," I say bitterly. "Like *that* could ever happen."

There's a gate in the barbed-wire fence where trucks come and go. Newly energized, we sprint for it.

I don't want to kill Laska anymore. When you're on the run, there are enough ways to die.

And we just narrowly escaped one of the worst.

8

TORI PRITEL

Malik proves that a point can be interesting and gross at the same time.

"If we went into that wood chipper, what would have happened when the cops tried to take DNA samples of the goo that was left of us? We'd be a perfect match for four criminals who are supposed to be locked up in jail."

Amber rolls her eyes. "At least the caterpillars didn't get you."

He glares at her. "Big talk from the person who got us into this mess. You'd better hurry, Laska. There are still a few people in Denver who don't know that we're clones."

Amber's tight-lipped. "Okay, that was a mistake. But it was a chance worth taking. If it had worked, Osiris would be out of business, and we wouldn't be sneaking around and looking over our shoulders."

I'm not so sure how I feel about putting Osiris "out of business." That would mean my parents would end up in jail for being a part of it. I obviously hate what they did to me, but I can't bring myself to hate them. I know they loved me. They would have cried if I'd gone into that chopping machine—and not just because their experiment was down the drain.

We've been walking about twenty minutes, watching the dusk creep over the open fields.

Eli says what we've all been thinking, but haven't had the guts to say out loud: "It's getting dark. We're going to have to find a place to sleep."

"Oh, no problem," Malik says sarcastically. "We'll just check into one of these five-star hotels and order up room service."

"It doesn't have to be a hotel," Eli persists. "We just need shelter and a place to rest."

Amber squints and points. "I see some lights over there."

After another few minutes, we come to a neighborhood. There are tree-lined streets, and neat brick and adobe homes. It's the closest thing to Serenity we've seen since leaving, with a couple of major differences. First, all of

Serenity would fit into a few blocks here, minus the plastics factory, of course. And second, in Serenity, every home had a tree house, and a pool. These houses are smaller, and not quite as well kept. When poor Hector dented his garage door trying to teach himself to ride a bike, the damage was fixed by nightfall. Things aren't as perfect in the real world. Here every house has something at least a little bit wrong with it—a missing bulb, a loose curbstone, uncut grass, an oil-stained driveway, or a pile of folded newspapers on the front stoop.

Amber notices that too, despite the fading light. "What kind of person orders newspapers and just leaves them on the porch?"

Eli looks thoughtful. "Maybe they got really busy, so they haven't had time to read."

Malik is doubtful. "Too busy to see them? They probably trip over them every time they go in and out of the house."

"No, then the papers would be all ripped up," I muse. "It's almost like there's nobody living here." I know it must sound crazy that it takes so long to dawn on me. But we're four kids who never left Serenity, even overnight. "Vacation!" I exclaim.

Malik looks mildly interested. "What about it?"

"That's why the papers are piling up! The people are on vacation! This house is empty!"

Amber is getting excited. "So we can find a way in, and hole up while we figure out what we should do next."

Malik breaks into a big grin. "First dibs on the TV."

"First dibs on the shower," I chime in.

Eli looks worried. "I'd really love to avoid breaking and entering."

"I admire you for that," says Malik with a smile. "Tell you what—you sleep on the street. I'm looking forward to a nice warm bed."

"Come on, Malik. This is somebody's home. How about respect for other people's property?"

"How about respect for DNA?" he shoots back. "The guy I'm cloned from—you think he'd have a problem with breaking into this house? He'd probably steal everything that wasn't nailed down too. But I'm not going to do that because I'm too nice. You're welcome."

Amber rolls her eyes. "Shut up, Malik. I'm not thrilled about breaking in either. But sometimes you have to balance the bad thing you do for the good result you need. We need to get out of the open where we can be spotted. We need a real night's sleep. We need to eat something. Everything we need is inside that door."

Eli is unconvinced. "I can just imagine the people we're cloned from using excuses like that to justify what they do."

Sometimes it's easier to picture Eli as an exact genetic copy of a Good Samaritan than a criminal.

"We're not them," I soothe. "We're us. And we're just trying to survive. If people see four kids sleeping outside in some park, what do you think they'll do? Call the cops."

Eli nods reluctantly. "Fine. How do we get in?"

"Let's wait for it to get a little darker," I advise. "If this place is anything like Serenity, everybody minds everyone else's business. We'll wait till nobody can see what we're doing, and go in from the back."

We slip through the gate into the yard, and into a metal tool shed. The floor practically crawls with ants and beetles, and I hear a whimper from Malik. (For a big, tough guy, he's such a wimp about insects.) I pick up four flashlights. We can't use the lights of the house because we don't want the neighbors to know anybody's in there.

Once the sun is down, it gets dark pretty fast. It's time to make our move.

"So what happens now?" asked Malik. "Heave a rock through the back slider?"

I don't even answer him. I'm concentrating on the house, searching for a way in. I notice the upstairs windows first. It must be an artist thing—something about those windows is vaguely unbalanced. The sash sits a tiny bit higher in the one on the left. It's barely a quarter-inch difference, but to me it's glaringly obvious.

The window isn't open—there's no gap. But I'm willing to bet—if Serenity kids bet, which, of course, we don't—that it's closed but not locked. That's why it's slightly higher; there's no latch forcing it down.

So if I can get up there . . .

All at once, I see the path. It's as clear as if someone marked it in chaser lights: shinny up the drainpipe, sidestep to the roof of the screen porch, and then it should be handhold one, handhold two, handhold three—and you're in.

As I'm climbing, I try not to think about where this strange skill set comes from. My dad used to be a rock climber, but of course he's not really related to me. I'm probably cloned from a cat burglar—and a good one, too, to qualify for the Osiris experiment. (Which is obviously nothing to be proud of. Still, it could be a lot worse. One of the guys is a copy of the Crossword Killer.)

I was right. The sash raises easily. I shoot the others a triumphant grin. They seem amazed. I'm the opposite. As unsure of myself as I can sometimes be, I had total confidence in the way up and the way in. Go figure.

Once I crawl inside, it hits me: we are now officially criminals, just like the people who supplied our DNA. True, we've broken laws before in the course of our run for freedom. This feels different. We chose a house, and we busted in. I understand why we did it. It was even partly my idea. But I can't escape the sense that a corner has been turned.

You think too much, Torific. Do what you have to do.

I switch on my flashlight and take a quick look around. I'm in the bedroom of a girl about my age, all frills and pastel colors. It's a stab at my heart. This could have been my room before I traded dust ruffles and stuffed animals for art supplies and a studio in the attic. When I thought my parents were my real parents, and thanked my lucky stars that I lived in the town ranked number one in the country in almost every category. It's not that long ago, but it might as well be a different century.

I'd never go back to that ignorance. But I don't doubt that I was happy.

I shake myself, and hurry down to the back slider to let the others in. Our lights play over the living room. It's a modest house, nowhere near the luxury we were accustomed to in Serenity. But after what we've suffered in the past few days, it's like coming into port in a raging storm.

Malik follows his flashlight into the kitchen, and is soon

rummaging around the fridge.

Eli is disapproving. "Bad enough we break into their house. We shouldn't be stealing their food."

"Who are these people?" Malik demands. "Don't they eat?"

"They're on vacation," Amber supplies. "They're not going to leave food to spoil while they're away."

Malik has moved on to the freezer. "Jackpot!" he exclaims reverently. "Microwave pizza! Who's hungry?"

The simple answer—everybody. (Nearly getting killed gives you an appetite.)

We stuff ourselves with pizza and a box of Fig Newtons we find in the pantry. Malik chugs an entire bottle of Dr Pepper and opens one of Coke. Eli looks like every bite is choking him.

"Cheer up, boy scout," Malik advises, mouth full. "Hating your pizza isn't going to make it any less stolen."

"We're just doing what we have to," Amber argues, "to survive."

Malik takes a giant swig of his second drink. "How many chances did we ever get to eat as much junk food as we want without some hidden camera recording us, and Project Osiris making notes? Like pigging out makes you a criminal." He utters a long, rolling belch.

"There ought to be a law against *that*," I say.

Afterward, I stack up the plates and begin washing them off in the sink. Malik starts to say something, but I freeze him with a fierce look. "Bad enough we broke in and ate their food. I don't want these poor people to come home and find a big mess in their house."

"You're a saint," he agrees. "You must have been cloned from Joan of Arc."

We learn a few things about our "hosts" from the mail on their kitchen counter. They are the Campanella family, and the Denver suburb they live in is called Mountain View. One of the parents seems to be a teacher, since there's a bulletin from the Colorado Education Association. There's a magazine called *Sports Illustrated*, so somebody must a sports fan. Another, *TV Guide*, lists every show you can watch on television that week. I can't helping thinking how much thinner it would be if they published it for Serenity, where there's only one channel.

"Well, we know one thing about the Campanellas," Malik crows, holding up a large envelope covered with printed messages and a lot of exclamation points. "They're dumb. This says they might have won ten million dollars, and they didn't even bother to open it." He rips into the side with his index finger.

Eli is horrified. "That's somebody's mail!"

"And they're welcome to it," Malik agrees readily. "It's the ten million bucks I want." He sorts through the contents, his brow darkening. "There's no money in here!"

"They *might* have won ten million dollars," Amber reminds him. "They also might not have."

"The outside world stinks. All they do is get people's hopes up." He crumples the envelope into a ball and tosses it back onto the counter. "I'm going to grab a shower."

There are two bathrooms upstairs. The boys take one, and Amber and I take the other. It's only after we're clean that we realize how much our clothes aren't. We're still in our Serenity Day outfits from the night of our escape, and they're totally ripe. They've been wandering through the desert, riding in a boxcar, running from the Purples, and rolling in a Dumpster. And they're sap-, leaf-, and blood-spotted from our ride in the tree service truck.

"Well," Amber reasons, "you can't keep a low profile when you stink to high heaven."

Even Eli reluctantly agrees. Like it or not, we're going to have to "borrow" some clothes.

The Campanellas are a family of five and, between them, they have sweatshirts and jeans to fit everybody. The dad is a fair match for Malik, but the teenage son is quite a bit bigger than Eli, who looks skinny and lost in a baggy sweatshirt and jeans. I have the same problem with the younger daughter's stuff (she's at least a size and a half larger than me). Amber can make do with the older daughter's, although the clothes are tight, which has her worrying about her goal weight for a change.

"Right," Malik says sarcastically. "Because being a fugitive is fattening."

We also take backpacks from the kids, and an extra outfit each. By the process of first dibs, Malik ends up with a sparkly pink princess knapsack.

I can't hold back a smirk, and Amber practically giggles, which doesn't happen very often. "It looks good on you," she manages. "Very manly."

He glares at her. "You're talking to someone who's out ten mil, so watch it."

Eli leaves a note for the Campanellas: *We're very sorry about taking your things. We'll pay you back someday.*

"A little short on details," I observe.

"We can't very well tell them who we are and where to find us. And we can't leave them any money. We're going to need every cent we've got and more."

Malik is sprawled out on the bed beside the princess backpack, flipping channels on the TV. Suddenly, he sits bolt upright. "Guys—get over here!"

There on the screen is a picture of the rear façade of a four-story building and the alley below. It doesn't take us long to realize that we're looking at the Medical Arts building in downtown Denver—the window we climbed out of, and the Dumpster we landed in.

". . . *the young girl, who appeared to be in a disturbed condition, was being taken for psychological evaluation when three other young people engineered her escape. They rappelled down the side of this building using a fire hose and disappeared into the city. Police are investigating the sighting of four youths in a municipal services yard in Mountain View, but caution that they have not yet confirmed that these two incidents are related.*"

Another photograph appears on the screen—Amber, seated in a chair, in a dingy office.

"They took your picture!" I exclaim.

She's sheepish. "I guess I should have mentioned that."

"So everybody in Denver has seen the crazy girl who ran away from the cops?" Malik exclaims. "Yeah, that might be something we should know!"

". . . *police released this photograph, but withheld the girl's name. At a press conference early this evening, a spokesman was careful to point out that she has not been accused of any crime, and was never under arrest . . .*"

At that point, the screen shows a uniformed officer speaking to reporters. "*We're worried about this girl. She's just a kid and, based on the story she told, we have reason to believe that she's extremely troubled. Her so-called rescuers are no older than she is, and they seem to have no adult supervision. As you can see, they took some pretty crazy risks in order to get away. If anyone knows anything about these four kids, please call our tip line.*"

As the camera withdraws from him, we get a better view of the media and spectators gathered around. Standing in the background is a tall man in a plum-colored paramilitary uniform and beret. We recognize him immediately—Baron Vladimir von Horseteeth.

It's like the temperature in the bedroom drops thirty degrees. An icy shiver runs up and down my spine. None of us thought Project Osiris would give up the search, but we never expected the Purple People Eaters to be hot on our heels so quickly.

"I'm sorry, you guys," Amber murmurs. "It's all my fault."

"They would have figured it out anyway," I tell her. "They know we ditched their SUV at the place with all the buses."

"But we've got to leave town," Eli adds.

"Now?" asks Amber.

I feel my stomach tighten. I'm looking forward to the prospect of a night in a real bed in a real house.

Eli thinks it over. "I think we're better off lying low tonight. But tomorrow we have to move on." He turns to Amber. "And you need a haircut."

Amber is mystified. "What's my hair got to do with it?"

Eli points at the TV. "The whole world just saw a picture of a girl with long blond hair. So you need to be a girl with short dark hair."

Malik's hand shoots up. "Oh! Pick me! I want to do the haircut! I saw a Weedwacker in the shed!"

Amber sighs. "Okay, fine. But Tori's doing it, with real scissors!"

"The big question is," I say, quieting everybody down, "where are we going to go, and how are we going to get there?"

"I've been poking around," says Malik. "There's a Jeep Wrangler in the garage. Those must be the keys on that hook in the kitchen."

We all look to Eli, expecting him to protest, but he surprises us. "We'll take it. It's too dangerous on buses now that the police know to look for four of us. And sooner or later, the Campanellas will get it back."

"Great," I say. "It's all settled except for one thing—where are we going to go?"

"I've been thinking," he says slowly. "Maybe Amber had the right idea about going to the police."

"Right." Malik is bitter. "Because today was so fun."

Amber studies the carpet, her face flushed.

"I'm being serious," Eli tells her. "The cops didn't believe you about Osiris, but what if we had proof?"

"Our Clone Society of America membership cards?" Malik suggests.

"A witness."

"A witness?" Amber echoes. "The only witnesses are our parents. Even the Purples don't know everything."

"There's one other person," Eli insists. "My dad had a partner when he created Osiris. Tamara Dunleavy, the internet billionaire. She bailed out of the project before it got started, which means she isn't necessarily on our parents' side. She lives on a ranch near Jackson Hole, Wyoming." His dark eyes burn with that crazy intensity he gets sometimes. "I vote we go there."

Amber and I have been styling each other's hair since before kindergarten. But taking scissors to it obviously ratchets things to a new level. I clip slowly, a little at a time. You'd think I'm cutting off fingers for how dramatic she's being.

"I don't want to look like a cactus!"

"It's hair, Amber. It grows back."

By the time I'm through, she's got a short bob, kind of pixie-style, with bangs. It isn't exactly salon quality, but I have to say it's not awful.

The next order of business is the color. Turns out Mrs. Campanella doesn't dye her hair. It's looking like we're going to have to use boot polish when we find the dad's supply of that Just For Men stuff you brush into your beard. Twenty minutes later, Amber's own mother wouldn't recognize her. (I mean the person who pretended to be her mother, obviously.)

"Oh, wow," Amber moans, glued to her reflection in the mirror. "Wow."

I struggle to find something positive to offer. "Well, the good news is you're the total opposite of Amber Laska, which was the whole point, right?"

She nods. "Wow."

When we emerge from the bathroom, I announce grandly, "Presenting someone who looks nothing like the girl on the news tonight!"

It falls on deaf ears. Malik is passed out on the king-size

bed. Eli is slumped over the computer on the desk. Both are fast asleep.

I've never been so jealous of anyone in my whole life. Amber and I each choose a kid's bedroom and crash.

9

ELI FRIEDEN

Felix Frieden—Felix Hammerstrom—stands at the head of the table, his steely gray eyes every bit as cold as I remember them. He's under tight rein, but I can tell how mad he is. They're in the conference room of the Serenity Plastics Works, a factory that's supposed to be making traffic cones, but is really the headquarters of Project Osiris. Eleven whiteboards stand in a semicircle, each one covered in notes and photographs, telling the life story so far of eleven clones.

He slaps the pointer against my picture. "We gave them everything," he says with barely controlled fury. "The gift of Serenity—all the tools to overcome the criminality of their basic nature. And this is how they repay us."

Steve Pritel, Tori's "father," is almost in tears. "My Torific would never do this. She loves us, and I know we love her. It's the evil influence of one of the others." His eyes flash to Dr. Bruder, Malik's "father."

Dr. Bruder cocks a brow. "Aren't we getting a little emotional over something that is, after all, pure science? The whole purpose of the Osiris experiment is to determine if the subjects' immoral natures will overcome their Serenity upbringing. Now we have our answer. They've broken into a house, taken what they needed without a second thought. They're resourceful, ruthless, and fearless, with no loyalty to anyone but themselves. They have all the attributes of the DNA that created them, and they've shown that they won't hesitate to use those talents in ruthless pursuit of their goals."

"Are you saying," asks Mrs. Laska, "that the experiment is over?"

Dr. Bruder nods. "We may not be getting the answer we were looking for, but it's certainly an answer."

"You're all missing the point," comes a voice from the doorway. Everyone wheels. A tall, vitally energetic woman with piercing blue eyes and striking white hair enters the conference room and stands before them.

I've never met her, but I know her from pictures. She's Tamara Dunleavy, cofounder of and one-time partner in Project Osiris.

"You're not looking at the issues in the order of their

importance," she goes on, her authoritative voice resounding in the enclosed space of the conference room. "Who cares about your twisted little experiment? Don't you see? You have duplicated four of the worst people in human history, and unleashed them on the world!"

My numb hand slips out from under my chin, and I whack my face against the corner of the computer monitor—hard. I come awake with a start. Light floods the master bedroom through the venetian blinds. Morning. I must have spent the night hunched over the computer. My body feels it in every joint.

Malik is still asleep on the bed. I don't know where the girls are.

I shudder as my dream comes back to me. I never want to think about Felix Hammerstrom again, but that doesn't stop him from invading my head every night. I see his frozen face, which is the closest thing to parental love I'll ever know, and the photo of my dead mother, who never existed.

This is the first time the nightmares have included Tamara Dunleavy, though. It's already shaking my belief that going to find her is the right thing to do. How do we know that she won't turn us over to the police or, worse, the Purple People Eaters? After all, she helped develop Project

Osiris, which means at some point she must have believed that cloning criminal masterminds was a great idea.

Just before she didn't, that is.

So how will she react to us? For all we know, she really will consider us a menace to society. But as I wake up a little more and my head clears, I'm still convinced that going to her is a risk worth taking. She's the only person outside Serenity who can back up who and what we are.

As I get to my feet, I jostle the mouse, bringing the computer out of screen-saver mode. What I see on the monitor nearly stops my heart.

It's a pop-up alert from the airline that the Campanellas' flight from Honolulu arrived at Denver Airport six minutes early at 7:44 a.m. Checked luggage can be claimed on carousel 3.

I stare at the clock on the screen. It's 8:31. The Campanellas landed more than forty-five minutes ago! They could be home any minute!

"*Wake up!*" I bark at Malik. I must be yelling pretty loud because he jumps eight inches off the bed.

"What?"

"They're coming!" I babble.

"The Purples?"

"The Campanellas! The people who live here! Their

plane landed forty-five minutes ago! We've got to get out of here!"

Amber and Tori hear the yelling and come running in.

My first sight of the new Amber with hair shorter and darker than Tori's is so shocking that I momentarily forget the crisis that's almost upon us.

Malik is half-asleep and bleary-eyed. He stares at Amber. "Mrs. Campanella?"

"It's me, dummy!" Amber snaps. "What's going on?"

We fill them in, and the next few minutes are a mad scramble of kicking into shoes, and gathering up our freshly stolen backpacks. We snatch the keys from the kitchen hook, and race for the garage.

The girls pile into the back of the Jeep; Malik and I take the front, with me at the wheel. We try every button and switch, looking for the garage door opener, starting the wipers, the washers, high beams, and fog lights. Finally, Malik locates it rubber-banded to the sun visor. He presses the button, and the door begins to rise.

I watch it through the rear-view mirror. It reveals the last thing any of us want to see. A taxi is parked at the curb, and the Campanella family is piling out, retrieving their luggage. They stop what they're doing, and stare open-mouthed at their garage.

"Hang on!" I throw the Jeep into reverse and stomp on that gas pedal like it was a venomous spider. The car shoots backward down the drive, clipping one of the suitcases, which bursts open, hurling clothing up in the air. A Hawaiian grass skirt comes down on the windshield, and Malik tries to brush it aside with the windshield wipers.

The dad of the family is sprinting toward us now, bellowing in fury.

I stomp on the brake, throw the car into gear, and we take off with a squeal of tires. I have to swerve to avoid Mr. Campanella, and jump the curb, flattening his mailbox.

By the time we turn the corner out of sight, he's already on his cell phone.

"Calling the cops," Malik guesses.

I get up to speed on the main road, keeping my eyes peeled for a freeway entrance away from this neighborhood. "Listen, you guys," I toss over my shoulder. "In another minute, this car's license number is going out over the police radio as stolen. There's no way we can drive it to Jackson Hole."

Amber pounds the back of my seat. "We have to ditch it!"

"Not here!" Malik counters. "They're looking for the car, but they're looking for us too. We'll be four morons, wandering on random streets, just waiting to be arrested."

I make a snap decision. "The bus station."

"In downtown Denver?" This from Tori. "Isn't that too risky? There are more cops there than anywhere."

"Not necessarily," I counter. "We'll separate so they'll never see four of us together. They don't know what we look like, and they won't recognize Amber. Then it's on to Jackson Hole—by bus."

"There's only one problem," Tori muses nervously. "If they find the Jeep near the terminal, they'll know we left town on a bus. They can radio every driver, and ask about four kids."

"They won't find the Jeep near the bus station," Malik promises.

"What are you talking about? Of course they will!"

He grins. "Just get us to the bus station, and leave everything else to me."

I have absolutely no idea where I'm going, but the Jeep's navigation system is easy enough to follow, and soon we're headed downtown on the highway. I can't tell you it's a breeze. We spend most of the ride in stiff-necked misery, scouring the road for police cars. We even spot a couple. Luckily they're too far away to notice us.

At one point, we hear a siren, and I nearly drive up a

telephone pole. But it turns out to be an ambulance. False alarm.

When we reach downtown, the traffic thickens, and so does the tension. Pedestrians and fellow motorists can see right into our car. In my mind, our license plates are the size of billboards, pulsating with the neon message: *Stolen Car. Arrest These Kids.* If we're going to get caught, it's sure to happen here, and soon.

And then the bus station is looming on the right. "What now?" I ask Malik.

"Drop the girls here," he instructs. "We'll meet on the platform for the next bus to Jackson Hole."

Tori is anxious as they climb out of the Jeep. "What are you guys going to do?"

"We're going to find the worst neighborhood in Denver."

I'm pretty sure they think he's joking—which is what I think until he directs me through the narrow streets behind the terminal, carefully choosing each turn so that it will take us down a dirtier, more dilapidated, garbage-strewn block. Soon we see graffiti on the walls, security bars on the windows, and seedy-looking characters on every stoop and corner. I know everything seems kind of seedy compared with Serenity. But even by big city standards, this is pretty scary.

"Are you sure you know what you're doing?" I ask nervously. "This looks like a really dangerous place."

"Probably," Malik agrees, his voice nervous but determined. "But when you need to make a car disappear, it's where you want to be. Stop here, and don't turn off the engine."

"But why—?"

He shuts me up with a look. "Just follow my lead."

We get out of the car, leaving the keys in the ignition and the motor running, and begin to hurry up the block. By the time we reach the corner, there are already two figures circling the Jeep.

"They're going to steal the car!" I hiss.

"That's the whole idea," he intones. "By the time the cops find it, it'll be miles from the bus station, and we'll be long gone."

"Those poor Campanellas."

"What do you care?" he demands a little peevishly. "They already know their car is stolen. They watched us take it. What difference does it make if we keep it, or pass it on to the next crooks?"

Next crooks. My stomach sinks further. "I'd hate to meet the guy you're cloned from."

"He's old news," Malik scoffs. "He's rotting in jail somewhere. I'm the one you have to worry about. And I'm just starting to get the hang of the outside world."

Sometimes Malik scares me.

10

AMBER LASKA

The bus ride to Jackson Hole takes fifty years. At least, that's what it feels like. The real number is more like thirteen hours, which is bad enough. When you grow up in a town that can be crossed on foot in eight minutes, five hundred plus miles has no meaning for you.

We decide that it's too risky to sit together. The police are searching for a group of four, so traveling as solo kids seems the safest. At first I'm almost looking forward to it—some alone time to organize my thoughts, maybe even make a mental to-do list. But then I realize there'd be nothing to put on it. Ballet practice? Yeah, right. Homework? I'm not even in school. My goal weight? I haven't stepped on a scale since leaving Serenity. The things I worked so hard to keep under tight control before just aren't in my life anymore.

And the weirdest part? I don't even care. Compared to what we're facing out here—like finding Tamara Dunleavy, and learning the truth about ourselves—worrying about grades, or ballet, or a diet just seems dumb. It's like mourning my long blond hair that I've been growing for the past thirteen years. It needed to be gone. Too bad. We did what we had to do. End of story. My "mother" called it my crowning glory. Consider me uncrowned.

"Very womanly," was Malik's official opinion on the new me, delivered at the station in Denver. It's revenge for my crack about the princess backpack—which is currently riding in the baggage compartment under the bus even though it could easily fit in the overhead rack.

"Seems to me it's more manly *not* to get all bent out of shape over a little pink knapsack," I told him as he placed it in there among the giant suitcases and trunks.

"There's plenty of room for you down here too," was his reply.

Come to think of it, maybe I have one thing to put on my imaginary to-do list:

THINGS TO DO TODAY (ONE ITEM ONLY)

- Punch Malik in the face . . .

But that's not an option until we get to Jackson Hole.

Okay, fine. It's not really an option, period.

Oh, please get me off this bus!

My seatmate conked out on my shoulder ten minutes out of Denver, and is pressing me up against the window. I'm actually questioning whether I'm cloned from a real criminal. A true mastermind would have figured out a way to toss her out of the speeding bus a hundred miles ago.

I shouldn't complain. Tori is two rows behind me, and she's much worse off. The man next to her can't seem to believe that anybody sent a twelve-year-old alone on a thirteen-hour bus ride. She had to come up with this elaborate lie about how her parents are divorced, and she's on her way to visit her dad. The problem is she was so convincing that now the guy is peppering her with questions. If this keeps up, she's going to have to invent an entire life story. Maybe when this nightmare is over, she can write a book.

We were writing a book together in Serenity—a picture book for young children. Tori was going to be the illustrator. Funny what never occurred to us: that there hardly *were* any young children in our town. The only kids that mattered were the Osiris lab rats, and we were all in middle school.

I try to pass the hours by going over what little we know about Tamara Dunleavy. Now sixty-three years old, she's one of the richest women in the world. She started out a daring and brilliant computer hacker, but later founded VistaNet, the company that made her a billionaire. She's currently retired, living on a ranch somewhere outside Jackson Hole.

"Somewhere outside" might be the operative words here. I gaze at the endless miles passing by the window. We don't even know if we're going to be able to find her, or what kind of reception we'll get if we track her down. But we do know that she walked out on Project Osiris, which could mean that she objected to the idea of creating human beings just for the purpose of experiment.

Maybe—just maybe—she'll be on our side.

According to Tori, the scenery around Jackson Hole is supposed to be some of the most beautiful in the country. We have to take everybody's word for that. It gets dark before we get a chance to see anything. We pull into the bus station after midnight, and wander the main strip, taking in our surroundings. At least we're allowed to be four kids again. There's no way the Denver police followed us up here.

The town, Jackson, is nice. It's the first place we've seen

that's as neat and clean, up-to-date, and shiny-modern as Serenity. I can't even find a crack in the sidewalk or a single piece of litter. In school, my mother told us that our town was completely unique in that way. Lie number ten thousand, or maybe more.

One difference, though—Jackson seems to be all stores and restaurants, and most of the shops sell either ski equipment, fancy candles, or T-shirts.

"People here must be real dopes," Malik concludes. "They can't remember where they live unless it says 'Jackson Hole' on their clothes and coffee mugs."

"That's not it," Eli puts in. "People come here on vacation to go skiing. These shirts and things are souvenirs."

Vacation. Souvenirs. These are alien ideas to us. I have to say I'm not impressed. Life has big challenges, and deciding between the Jackson Hole steak knives and Ski Wyoming alpine bobblehead shouldn't be one of them.

"We're not going to find Tamara Dunleavy now," Tori points out with a yawn. "It's the middle of the night. We need a place to crash so we can go after her in the morning."

"How are we going to do that?" challenges Malik. "I don't think any of these stores went to Hawaii like the Campanellas."

We walk a little farther. After hours of sitting on the bus, it feels good to stretch our legs. The high-class shops and eateries thin out a little, giving way to the less fancy kind of places that we saw in Denver—convenience stores, burger joints, and something called a pawn shop, with a variety of unrelated objects in the window. You can't tell what kind of store it really is. I'm pretty sure they're not selling pawns, like in chess.

The farther we go from the center of the strip, the less Serenity-like it gets, until at last we come to a neon sign that reads: *MOTE*, which is really *MOTEL*, but the *L* is burned out. Underneath it says *Reasonable Rates*, which sounds like us, since we're running low on cash. It actually says *Reasonable Rats*, but that's only because the *E* fell off and is lying on the grass.

"I don't want *any* rats, even reasonable ones," grumbles Malik.

"I thought your problem was bugs," I needle him.

Malik scowls. For a guy who makes a lot of jokes, he has no sense of humor.

Tori comes up with a plan. I take our money and head into the small office. The clerk, who doesn't seem that much older than me, has been sleeping, no doubt about it.

"A room for one night, please."

He blinks at me, trying to wake up. "How old are you?"

"Fifteen," I say, bumping up my age by two years. Credit to Tori for choosing me for this mission, since I'm the oldest girl. "My mom gave me the money to pay. She's just parking the car. We've been on the road all day."

For a minute, he looks like he's going to wait until I produce "Mom." I feel like he can hear my heart racing. If we can't convince one semiconscious teenager that there's nothing fishy about us, we might as well go back to Serenity right now.

In the end, the idea of going back to sleep is stronger than his curiosity about me. He comes up with a form to fill out, and slides a key across the counter. I give him ninety dollars, which doesn't seem like a very reasonable "rat," but I'm hardly an expert at the price of things in the outside world.

"Thanks," I say, and head out to sneak myself and my friends into room 12.

The "Mote" is kind of cheesy, but as we walk to our unit, we pass a glassed-in room designated *Guest Services.* Inside we can see a coin-operated washer and dryer, an ironing board, a battered treadmill, and a computer and printer on a folding card table marked *Business Center.*

"Internet." Eli's eyes light up. "You guys go to the room.

I'll see if I can find an address for Tamara Dunleavy."

Room 12 is smallish and not in the greatest shape. But this is our second night in a row with actual beds, a working TV, and a real bathroom. Luxury.

We watch a news broadcast and discover that the outside world has more important things to worry about than the missing crazy girl in Denver and her three friends who broke her out of custody.

I let out a sigh of relief. It was *my* screw-up that got us wanted by the Denver police in the first place. It would be awful to be caught, but even worse if it's my fault. I was *so sure* talking to that cop would solve all our problems. For all my lists and organization, I was the one who did the stupid, impulsive thing that almost sank us.

THINGS TO DO TODAY (AND EVERY DAY)

- Look before you leap!

But we seem to have lucked out. Nobody's searching for us anymore except the Purples—and they have no way of knowing where we are.

I hope.

Malik is almost insulted that the manhunt is over. "The cops are such idiots. They've got four criminal masterminds on the loose and they don't even know it."

Tori stares at him. "You're kidding, right? This makes our lives a million times easier. Can you imagine trying to find Tamara Dunleavy if we didn't dare show our faces in public?"

"And we're *not* criminal masterminds," I add pointedly. "We just got our DNA from them."

Malik shrugs. "Stealing cars, running from cops, busting into a house—if you ask me, we're putting together a pretty good rap sheet."

Tori glances at her watch. "What's keeping Eli? You don't think the desk clerk caught him?"

"That guy?" I snort. "I guarantee he's dead to the world."

"You know Frieden and computers," Malik adds. "He's probably all nerded out, surfing and downloading and reprogramming, having the time of his life."

When Eli finally turns up half an hour later, though, his expression is grim. "I can't find Tamara Dunleavy."

"But everything we read says she lives around here," I protest.

"I'm sure she does," Eli agrees. "But there's nothing more than that—no address, no phone number. Not even a hint, like north of town, or near a certain mountain or river. Turns out you can be 'unlisted,' where your information stays private. It would be pointless in Serenity, where everybody knows everybody else. But here, rich people try to protect their privacy."

Malik shakes his head in disgust. "That makes no sense. What's the point of being rich if you can't show it off?"

"I hope you never get rich," I tell him.

Tori looks thoughtful. "Just because she's unlisted doesn't mean she's invisible. The local people must know about her—where she lives and places she goes. We'll have to ask around."

There's a new desk clerk at the motel when we leave that morning. When I hand in the key, I say, "We're going. My mom's just loading the car."

This clerk is an older woman, but she doesn't seem any more interested in the clientele than the sleepy teenager who took my money last night. She gives me an absent "Have a nice day."

"Mom wanted me to ask you," I forge on. "She's heard that Tamara Dunleavy has a ranch around here somewhere. Is that true?"

The woman looks blank. "Tamara who?"

"Dunleavy," I repeat. "You know, the internet billionaire."

She shrugs. "Never heard of her."

We have a very economical breakfast of toast and cereal at a diner. Why does everything we eat have to be unhealthy just because we're fugitives? Can't outlaws like vegetables?

Eli tries the waitress. "Does Tamara Dunleavy ever come in here? It would be cool to meet somebody so rich and famous."

The waitress thinks it over. "Tamara Dunleavy—didn't she play Penny on *The Big Bang Theory*?"

"No, she founded a company called VistaNet. She's a billionaire."

"We get a lot of celebrities here," the waitress replies, "but mostly during ski season. Zac Efron came in with his new girlfriend once and he was so nice. And Lady Gaga broke her ankle snowboarding last year, but that was at one of the resorts. My brother is an EMT, and he got a great selfie with her in the ambulance."

We exchange bewildered glances along the counter. Zac Efron? Lady Gaga? Who are they and what do they have to do with a scientific theory about the origin of the universe? What is she talking about?

We can't ask, because I think we're supposed to know. The outside world is different from Serenity, but this is *really* different.

Eli takes a paper out of his pocket and carefully unfolds it. It's a photograph of Tamara Dunleavy that he's printed from her Wikipedia page. "This is what she looks like."

The waitress's painted eyebrows go up. "You know what? I think I *have* seen her." She turns and holds the picture out to the short-order cook. "Karl, do you recognize this lady?"

The counterman glances over. "Oh, yeah, sure—everybody knows her."

"She comes in here?" I ask eagerly.

"Nah, not here. Strictly high-class, this one, money out the wazoo. A real do-gooder, up to her neck in every charity. Always saving something—the whales, the children, the rainforest, whatever's popular that week. Who wants to know?"

"My grandma grew up with her," Tori replies glibly. "Any idea where she lives? Grandma asked me to drop by and say hi."

The man gestures helplessly with his spatula. "Who knows? Pick a mountain, pick a mansion. Those fancy types love the nosebleeds."

As we leave the luncheonette, I sidle up to the others. "What's a wazoo?"

"It must be some kind of bank account," Malik guesses.

So we go to the bank, repeating all that stuff about Tori's grandmother to the manager. "I think she's one of your Wazoo clients," Tori adds helpfully.

"I'm sorry, but we're not permitted to give out information on our depositors." He looks like he's having a hard time keeping a straight face. Okay, so maybe wazoo isn't a bank account. By the time I learn everything I need to know about the world outside Serenity, I'll be a very old clone.

We try the post office and several more stores without much succcss. A few of the people we talk to recognize the picture, especially the ones in the more expensive stores. We pick up a smattering of information, but nothing really helpful: she rides around in a steel-gray chauffeur-driven Bentley; she's a good tipper, although not as good as the Hollywood types; no matter how dressed up she is, she always wears sneakers.

"Great," grumbles Malik, dropping himself to a bench on the main drag. "A rich lady in sneakers. That really narrows it down."

I feel a kind of helpless frustration that we're floundering like fish out of water. There should be a more systematic way of going about this. In Serenity, I was busier than the other kids, and I got everything accomplished by being *organized.* Jackson may be bigger than our hometown, but it's not a huge city like Denver. It can't be that hard to find a famous billionaire in a chauffeur-driven car.

And then I'm staring right at it. The largest building on the strip is the Jackson Convention Center. The sign that stands at the curb reads:

WELCOME
TETON COUNTY CHARITABLE SOCIETY

"Look!" I exclaim, pointing.

"Big deal," snorts Malik. "We're here to find Tamara Dunleavy, not paint the orphanage."

"Malik, you can be so dumb sometimes. Don't you remember what the cook said? She's a do-gooder! If this is a meeting of the local charities, she must be a part of it somehow. I bet she's in that convention center right now."

"It's worth a try," Eli decides. "The worst we can be is wrong."

As we approach the three-story building, four sets of

eyes see it at the same time—a steel-gray Bentley sedan in the parking lot. The Wyoming license plate reads *VISTA*.

"The company she founded is called VistaNet," Eli whispers.

Behind the tinted glass, a liveried chauffeur sits at the wheel, reading a book.

The pieces are clicking into place—a charitable society, a chauffeur-driven Bentley, VistaNet. I feel better, more in control. We're thinking methodically, not just grasping at straws.

We step into the ultra-modern chrome and glass lobby. A floor-to-ceiling board lists the day's events. The Charitable Society is meeting in the Gillette Ballroom, which is right on the main level.

We get there to the sound of applause from within. A moment later, the doors open and people begin to emerge, chatting among themselves as they head for the exit. Eli takes out his picture of Tamara Dunleavy and we all compare the passing faces with the photograph from Wikipedia. No matches.

The stream of attendees slows to a trickle. We exchange agonized glances. Could we have been mistaken about this? After the car and the chauffeur and everything?

Mustering my courage, I peer in the open door. There are still a few stragglers gathered around the podium. My heart sinks. No internet billionaire.

Finally, a large woman in an enormous orange muumuu steps out of the way, and I see her. The hair is white, swept back from a face that seems surprisingly youthful, with piercing eyes that are a brilliant shade of blue. She wears a charcoal-gray business suit, and on her feet, bright white sneakers fresh out of the box. The only indication that this person is enormously wealthy is her earrings, which feature diamond studs the size of dimes.

"Nice zombies," Malik whispers.

Tamara Dunleavy.

11

ELI FRIEDEN

It's her!

My hand is shaking so badly that I can't see the picture to make the positive identification. But we all recognize her.

Tamara Dunleavy, who collaborated with Felix Hammerstrom to create Project Osiris and then backed out at the last minute for reasons nobody knows. The only person outside Serenity who will understand who we are and how we came to be.

The rush of exhilaration I feel is so overwhelming that my step wobbles a little because I'm weak in the knees. We started out utterly clueless in the real world. Yet we've succeeded in taking a single name from the internet and locating this person hundreds of miles from where we were. I'm proud of us, but mostly, I'm filled with hope that the dream of some kind of future for us isn't completely impossible. If we can find this human needle in a haystack the size of America, then we're capable of opening any door.

I probably would have stood out there forever, frozen in the moment. But Malik gives me a gentle shove, and the four of us half walk, half stumble into the Gillette Ballroom.

Ms. Dunleavy hasn't noticed us yet. She's still bidding farewell to the last few members of her audience. One by one, they file out and we begin our approach.

I'm too tongue-tied to speak. It's Tori who finds her voice first. "Tamara Dunleavy?"

The founder of VistaNet turns in our direction. "Yes?"

A lot of adults outside Serenity have a kind of impatient attitude toward kids—like we're unimportant and they're afraid we'll waste their valuable time. She isn't like that at all. She gives us her full attention as we approach. In fact, we're about ten feet away when her eyes widen and fix on me.

"Do you know me?" I ask timidly.

"No," she replies. "It's just that, for a moment there, I thought you were someone else. Now, what can I do for you ladies and gentlemen?"

"Well—" Where to begin? We've been working toward this moment, anticipating it. Yet we've never really talked about what we'll say when it happens. "We know you were one of the creators of Project Osiris."

She looks shocked, but recovers quickly. "I think you must have me confused with someone else."

Tori steps forward. "Please. We saw the piece on the internet. It said Tamara Dunleavy, founder of VistaNet. That's you."

Her nervous laugh is in sharp contrast to the confident ease she was showing moments before. "You can't believe everything you read on the internet. When you're in my position, you'd be amazed where your name turns up sometimes."

"Like next to Felix Hammerstrom?" puts in Malik.

She shrugs. "I knew Felix. Brilliant social scientist. Maybe a little ahead of his time."

"He's my father," I interrupt. "At least, the closest thing to a father you get when you're—like me."

All the color drains from her face. It's clear that she's putting two and two together. We're the right age; we know about the project; we know about Hammerstrom. This must be her first inkling that the Osiris experiment went ahead even after she dropped out.

I say it outright to eliminate any possible misunderstanding. "It's us. *We're* Project Osiris, just like you and my dad planned it out—clones of criminal masterminds, not quite human. Freaks."

Ms. Dunleavy is deathly quiet. "How can you say such an insane thing about yourselves?"

Amber speaks up. "In Serenity, they told us honesty was the most important quality while they were lying to us about everything else. Please don't do that too."

"We need your help," I add. "We tried the police, but they didn't believe us. You're the only person who can back up our story."

"But I can't—"

"The Purples—the Surety are after us," I forge on, hoping to break through her resistance. "They nearly caught us in Colorado. If they drag us back to Serenity, we'll never get another chance to have real lives. If that happens, they *win*!" I take a deep breath and play my trump card. "You quit Osiris because you saw how wrong it was. You couldn't stop them then. Maybe you can stop them now."

Her face, still pale, turns stern, her expression closed. "I repeat: I have no idea what you're talking about."

Malik glowers. "Listen, lady, it's not just us. There are six more back in Happy Valley who don't even know the mess they're in." His voice cracks. "Not to mention the good kid who got killed trying to escape with us!"

Ms. Dunleavy is visibly shaken, but she sticks to her story. "I'm so sorry. I can see that you've been through a terrible experience and you really believe what you're saying. But it just doesn't have anything to do with me. Now, if you'll excuse me . . ."

She speaks with the authority and finality of someone who's used to being the boss. It's a weird moment. We know she's lying and she knows we're telling the truth, but there's nothing else to be said on the subject. I wait for Malik to argue, or Tori to plead, or Amber to lay a guilt trip. I wait for myself to say something, *anything*—even "Liar, liar, pants on fire!" But none of us offers a word. We just watch her walk away, taking with her all our hopes.

"She's some piece of work," Malik growls as soon as she's out of sight. "No way she's never heard of Project Osiris. She practically lost her lunch when you said the name!"

"I don't think she realized until now that Osiris really happened," I suggest. "She must have thought the whole thing was scrubbed when she quit. I guess she doesn't know my dad as well as she thinks she does. Everything has to be his way or no way."

"I don't care!" Amber exclaims bitterly. "If she helped dream up Osiris, she's a terrible person. Maybe a notch better than our parents, because she at least had the decency to bail out. But she's still in it up to her neck!"

Tori nods. "Did you see her staring at Eli? She knows who he's cloned from. I'll bet she thought she was looking at the guy."

I feel a deep dread that I must be a dead ringer for Bartholomew Glen. *That* was the expression on her face—that she'd just found herself eye to eye with the Crossword Killer.

"She was staring at all of us," Amber puts in, "although she never looked at me straight on. It's almost like she was peering over my shoulder at something behind me."

Malik is surprised. "You know, I thought that too. She's such a bad liar that she can't even face you while she's doing it."

"Actually," Tori muses, "she's a pretty *good* liar. If I didn't already know she was guilty, she would have convinced me."

"Fine," sighs Malik. "She's a fantastic liar who happens to have an eye tick which makes her look at people right here." He raises his index finger to a spot on his muscular neck just below his left ear.

"You know," Tori observes, "you do have a little bump there."

"Yeah, and you're a supermodel," Malik shoots back.

"Seriously—feel it."

So he does, and finds something just far enough back to be out of sight in a mirror. "Is that a pimple?"

"It's just a birthmark," I assure him. "You've always had it."

"Only"—Tori frowns—the expression she wears when she's noticing something no one else can see.

Malik is worried now. "What is it?"

"My dad had knee surgery when he was in college," she explains. "The scar's totally gone. All that's left is a faint little line, barely even visible. You've got a line like that through the middle of your birthmark."

"You're saying I had—*neck surgery*?" Malik sputters.

"Maybe. A long time ago." Tori's attention shifts to Amber. "And you have it too."

I gawk, squinting for focus. Tori's right! There's no bump, but Amber has a tiny, faded scar, barely visible, in the exact same spot as Malik's!

Well, that does it. We must seem pretty strange, because we're standing in a circle, staring at one another's necks. We all have it—an ancient scar, long healed, about an inch below the ear.

Amber has the strongest reaction. "Take it out! Take it out *now*!"

I'm mystified. "Take *what* out?"

"Don't you see?" she demands. "The invisible barrier around Serenity! This must be what made it work—a tiny receiver in our heads that made us sick every time we got close to leaving town. They did surgery on us, probably when we were babies! They cut us open and put some kind of chip inside!"

It's not a pleasant thought, but what other explanation could there possibly be? Identical scars in identical places—conveniently just out of view. And maybe Malik's shows because his implant—or whatever it is—wasn't stuck in deep enough.

Malik covers his skeeved-out expression by glaring at Amber. "How can we take it out? You've got a zipper?"

"I don't care! It's a clone thing and I want it gone!"

"What if we—you know—*need* it?" Tori asks in a worried tone. "What if, whatever it is, it's keeping us alive somehow?"

"Impossible," I counter. "We all did the research on clones. Except for how we started out, we're totally human."

Malik has a different concern. "Do you think the Purples can use whatever it is to track us? Like a GPS?"

"I doubt it," I reply. "If that was true, we never could

have made it this far. They would have scooped us up way back in Denver."

Tori nods. "So that's what it *isn't*. How do we find out what it *is*?"

Malik shrugs. "We can't. The thing's inside us. We can't get at it without a doctor."

Amber reaches over to a nearby table and picks up a small staple gun from atop a stack of posters. She brings the gun up to her neck and fires a staple into the skin near the bump.

Tori stifles a scream. "Amber, what are you doing? You're *bleeding*!"

Amber dabs at her wound with the corner of the tablecloth. "Well, what do you know? I guess I'm going to have to see a doctor."

12

AMBER LASKA

Okay, I admit it. It hurts a lot more than I expected it to.

Not only that, but the nurse in the ER looks at the others like they did it to me. The last thing we need is for someone to call the cops on us.

"It's my own fault," I say sheepishly. "We were putting up posters and my neck got itchy. I guess I forgot I was holding the staple gun."

"It must have gone in pretty deep," she observes, taking note of the blood trickling down to my collar.

Tell me about it. It feels like two spears have been plunged into the side of my head. Worse, I'm beginning to feel a little dizzy, although I don't mention that to the nurse. I want medical attention, but only to a certain degree. Passing out and being admitted to the hospital is definitely *not* on my to-do list for the day.

Then she starts asking a lot of nosy questions about my parents, and their jobs, and what health insurance they have. And when I point out that *I'm* the one who's injured, not my mom or dad, she confesses that all this is so the hospital can get *paid* for treating me.

"You mean," I challenge, "I'm sitting here, bleeding through staple holes in my neck, not seeing a doctor, because of *money*?"

This seems to fluster her. "It's just that, well, you have no insurance card, so we'll need to speak to a parent or guardian in order to get an ID number."

Even with Project Osiris, there are still times when Serenity makes a whole lot more sense than the world around it.

"I don't know about any of that! I just want to get the staple out!"

My frustration bubbles over but that might actually work in my favor, because she assumes I'm delirious with pain.

"Well, I suppose your parents can take care of the paperwork when they come to pick you up." She hesitates. "Your parents *will* be coming to pick you up, won't they?"

"What do you think?" I sigh.

She says she'll call me when it's my turn to see the doctor.

I get no relief in the waiting room. Tori and Eli resume their lecture on the subject of "Why would you do such a crazy thing?"

"Don't you think we should know what we've been carrying around in our bodies all these years?" I demand.

Tori is angry at me. "Doctors make appointments, Amber. You didn't have to maim yourself!"

"It's called the emergency room for a reason," I counter. "This is an emergency. And while the doctor's digging out the staple, he'll be like, 'Oh, hey, what's this other thing under your skin?'"

Only Malik seems to approve. "Good idea. It'll seem less suspicious if the guy thinks he's finding it on his own."

It's the first compliment I've gotten from Malik since . . . well, it might be the only compliment I've gotten from Malik. Or maybe he just enjoys watching me suffer.

As we wait, the bleeding stops.

"The spot on your neck is turning black-and-blue, though," Tori observes worriedly.

I have a giddy vision—another to-do list:

THINGS TO DO TODAY (UNPRIORITIZED)

- Fire industrial staple into neck (0.1 seconds)

I chuckle out loud at my own imagined joke.

Tori stares at me. "What could you possibly have to laugh about?"

Before I can answer, the nurse reappears. "You're up, honey."

The doctor is young and super-busy, so he doesn't question my itchy-neck story. He numbs me with some local anesthetic and removes the staple through a small incision. Then he pauses, puzzled, and says the words I've been waiting for:

"What's this . . . ?"

He reaches in with tweezers and pulls out something the size of a tiny, flat pill. "Curious." He examines it under a microscope and I lean in to share the view.

It's a miniature computer chip encased in clear plastic coating.

"What is it?" I ask.

He dabs some antibiotic ointment onto the wound and covers it with a square bandage. "I've never seen anything like this before," he says, frowning. "Maybe your mother should come in for this conversation."

"She's not here," I reply. "My friends and I were putting up posters when I had the, uh, accident. They brought me straight here."

"It looks like some kind of electronic tag," he muses.

"Tag?"

"My fiancée works for the Forest Service. They track animal migration with chips like this. But no one would use it on a child."

Clearly, the doctor has never been to Serenity, New Mexico. Animals; clones; what's the difference?

"The location is also strange," he goes on. "At the base of the skull, any implant would be close enough to interact with the body's nerve and pain centers."

Right—strange. Unless the goal is to trigger an attack of agony and nausea so intense that your escaping clones are too sick to go on. There's no place like home.

The doctor is starting to look impatient. His beeper is going off about every eight seconds, and the nurse has been peering in through the curtain, making hurry-up gestures. "You need to see your regular physician tomorrow to have the dressing changed."

"Thanks." I pluck the chip from his tweezers. "A souvenir," I explain.

He's too harried to care. He's already signaled the nurse to bring in the next victim.

While she's otherwise occupied, I sprint past Admitting, grab the others, and get out of there. It isn't Serenity-style honesty. But if they expect me to wait around for my parents to fill out paperwork, it's going to be a long night for all of us.

The minute I step out of Walgreens, Malik snatches the bag from my arms, pokes through the contents, and comes up with a box cutter. "Oh, no, you don't. You're not using that on me!"

"It has a razorblade," I tell him. "The sharper it is, the less it's going to hurt."

"How come you get to see a real doctor and the rest of us have to have meatball surgery?" he demands.

Eli is patient. "Because if four kids in a row troop into emergency with the same chip in their necks—all from out of town, no parents, no ID—people are going to start asking questions. And we don't have any answers—none that we can give them, anyway."

I show them the rest of my purchases: rubbing alcohol, Neosporin, a towel, tweezers, Band-Aids, and—

"Hemorrhoid cream?" Tori queries. "For our necks?"

"It's a numbing agent," I explain.

"Yeah, for people's butts!" Malik points out.

"Just trust me, okay? The pharmacist says it's the strongest you can get without a prescription. I didn't want to go into too much detail."

We decide to do the deed in a secluded park at the edge of downtown. I say this is for privacy, but I'm secretly thinking it will be good to be near the creek just in case there's a lot of blood to wash off. We're cloned from criminals, not surgeons.

As we dump our backpacks and establish our "operating room" at a picnic table by the water, another to-do list appears before me:

THINGS TO DO TODAY (UNPRIORITIZED)

- Carve up friends (unknown duration)

"I'll go last," Malik volunteers.

A tower of courage.

Eli puts on a brave face, but he's sweating like a horse as I rub hemorrhoid cream over the scar on his neck. Trust me, he can't be more scared than I am. My hands tremble as I pour alcohol on the box cutter.

This needs to be done, I tell myself. *So just do it.*

Numbing agent or not, Eli winces when the razor-blade pierces his skin, but he doesn't cry out. I make a tiny U-shaped cut right below the faded scar. I wasn't expecting the rush of blood. I try not to panic. The towel sops all that up.

"You okay?" I ask Eli.

"Peachy," he replies in a strained voice. "Just get it over with."

Next I dip the tweezers in the alcohol and start digging around inside the hole I made. I don't know if it's the tweezers or me, but it's hard to get a grip on such a little thing.

I'm sweating worse than Eli now, and even Tori looks gray in the face knowing she's next. Malik is on the bench, studying his sneakers. He doesn't even glance in our direction.

All at once, I feel something solid between the tweezers' tips. I get a good hold and draw out the chip. It's covered in pink ooze, but otherwise a perfect match for mine.

I sop up the blood again, clean the wound with alcohol, and slather it with Neosporin. Then I slap the bandage on, sealing it as tight as I can. "Done," I tell him in a shaky voice.

He slides away from me down the bench, making room for Tori. Apparently, standing up is not an option.

But within a few minutes, he's back to normal. "You're the worst doctor in the world," he tells me.

I manage a watery grin. "You're welcome."

Tori's "surgery" goes about the same as Eli's—a little less blood, although I have a harder time finding the chip to pull it out. She hangs tough through the whole thing, silent, her jaw clenched. I'm proud of her. She's the youngest, and artsy, but she's as strong as any of us. It makes perfect sense if you think about what we come from.

Then it's Malik's turn.

"You know, maybe I'll just leave mine in," he muses casually. "It's not like we have to escape from Serenity anymore."

He's trying to sound nonchalant, but he looks absolutely terrified.

"Come on, Malik," Eli says gently.

"And the transmitter that was generating the field is gone too—"

"It has to come out," I interrupt. "As long as it's still inside you, it'll always be a weakness our parents might be able to use against us one day."

As a patient, he's as cooperative as a panther with a thorn in its paw. Eli and Tori have to hold his head steady or I might cut his throat by mistake.

Or maybe it wouldn't be by mistake.

We finally shove the towel in his mouth and make him bite down on it just to shut him up. And still he's jerking around so badly that splattered blood droplets are getting all over the three of us. When it's done, we have to go down to the water and take turns helping one another clean up as best as we can.

It's a big job and a messy one. The stains come off our skin easily enough, but our clothes look bad, especially up around the collar. As for the towel—it's a write-off. Good thing the weather's warm, or we'd all have pneumonia, because we're pretty wet.

I take the four tiny electronic chips out of my pocket. "How about a watery grave for this stuff?"

Tori has a point. "Maybe we should keep it for evidence."

Eli shrugs. "Chips like that come out of every electronic toy. We'd never prove what they do or even that they came from us."

Malik nods as vigorously as he can with a sore neck. "Pitch 'em."

"Maybe we should say a few words," Tori says. "After all, this is the last piece of Serenity that was a part of us."

The pause that follows means we all know how wrong

that is. The portion of us that doesn't come from four horrible criminals will always be Serenity.

Malik breaks the silence by whacking the back of my hand. The four chips go flying and disappear into the water.

"Rest in pieces," he growls.

Eli's first to turn back to the picnic table. He freezes. "Hey!"

Someone's there—a man in sunglasses. He's got the backpacks, and he's rifling through our stuff! My first notion is that he's probably one of those poor homeless people like we saw in Denver. But he's well dressed, with a dark suit and one of those blinking cell phone headpieces attached to his ear.

"Get away from there!" Malik roars.

He, Eli, and Tori are already charging up the embankment. I'm a half step behind them, my wet jeans slowing me down. The thief sees us coming and starts away. We're younger, but he's drier, and in good shape for an older guy.

As I run, I look down and am shocked to see the box cutter in my hand. I must have taken it out of my pocket without thinking. Do I actually plan to cut this guy if I can catch him? It's the most un-Serenity notion imaginable; it has to come from my DNA.

I drop the box cutter like it's burning my hand and

devote all my energy to speed. I come up behind Eli and Malik, but I can't pass them because the picnic table is in the way. The guy is almost to the paved path. If he gets that far, he's as good as on the street and gone. We can't very well take him down in the middle of town—not if we want to keep a low profile.

Mustering all my ballet training, I get one foot on the bench, the other on the table, and then I'm airborne. I even do a grand jeté on the way—old habits are tough to break. The ballet move vaults me right up to the thief. My front foot gets tangled with his two fleeing ones. We both go down—me rolling across the soft grass; him sprawling through the underbrush. There's a *thwack* as his head hits the base of a tree.

We scramble up to prevent him from running away, but that turns out to be unnecessary. He's not moving.

"Is he dead?" pants Tori.

I lean down close to the face. "He's still breathing."

"Great," says Malik. "He can testify at our trial. And when they bring out the evidence, everyone's going to know I had a princess backpack!"

"Who do you think he is?" Tori wonders.

Eli shrugs. "If he's a crook, he's a lot higher class than the ones they have in Denver."

Malik is going through the man's suit coat. "If he's a crook, he's a pretty lousy one. He didn't steal anything."

"We don't really have a whole lot to steal," Eli reminds him.

"Wait—here's something." Malik comes up with a set of car keys. The winged B logo of a Bentley gleams from the fob.

"*That's* why he looks familiar!" Tori exclaims. "It's Tamara Dunleavy's driver!"

At the end of the path, we can see the aristocratic nose of the big car parked on the street.

Malik is confused. "Why would a billionaire send her driver to rip off our stuff?"

"To find out about us," I conclude. "I never believed for a second that she knows nothing about Project Osiris, and here's the proof!"

"If that's true," Tori muses, "why didn't she just ask us when we were standing right in front of her? Why send a guy to go through our bags?"

"Osiris is a crime," I reply. "She doesn't want to admit she had anything to do with it."

"I don't like it," Eli says nervously. "She's rich and powerful, and we're a danger to her because of what we know."

"Do you think she'd try to hurt us?" asks Tori.

"I wouldn't put anything past someone who could dream up Project Osiris," Eli replies grimly. "But she wouldn't even have to. She could turn us over to the Purples. Or have us arrested."

"On what charge?" I demand.

Malik indicates the unconscious chauffeur. "How'd you like to have to prove to the cops that we didn't attack him?"

"We have to get out of Jackson," Eli decides. "Fast."

"Oh, right," snorts Malik. "We're on foot and we've got no money. An eight-year-old on a scooter could run us down, no problem."

I take his wrist and shake it so that the car keys jingle.

Tori's wide-eyed. "Steal her car?"

"She helped create Osiris," I reason. "She owes us. The cost turns out to be one Bentley."

13

MALIK BRUDER

We're in the Bentley, headed out of town, with me behind the wheel. Yeah, that's right—I know how to drive. Not just Frieden. Back in Serenity, when we were planning our escape, we both taught ourselves on video games. It just happens that, so far, Frieden has hogged all the driving.

This is my first try, but it's all good. Hey, for a new driver, a Bentley isn't a half-bad car to break yourself in on. Glove leather seats practically form to your butt. The engine purrs like a kitten, with a ride as smooth as silk. The dashboard reminds me of a spaceship's control panel. There's even a touch screen with full internet, which is how we know that one of these costs $275,000, give or take, depending on the options—like internet, so your passengers have no trouble finding out how much you paid for the car. No sense being rich if nobody's jealous.

Tamara Dunleavy's rich—although now I guess she's technically poorer by one Bentley. But to her, that's a drop in the bucket. Having a billionaire mad at you is almost as scary as having the Purples mad at you—anybody that wealthy and powerful has to be considered a bad enemy. We can't know exactly what her intentions are, but she already sent her driver to spy on us. And when we knocked him out and stole the car, we can't have bumped ourselves up on her list of BFFs.

That's why Eli reaches over and tunes the radio to a news station.

I'm disgusted. "You're kidding, right? We have satellite radio, DirecTV, streaming web video, and you want to listen to AM?"

"AM is where we're going to hear that the police are looking for a stolen Bentley," he explains. "If they start talking about roadblocks, it's time to ditch the car."

"And walk across Wyoming?" Amber asks incredulously.

"It's better than being caught," Eli says firmly.

"But not much better," I add. "I really love this car."

So we listen to the news. An hour goes by. Nothing.

In the rearview mirror, I see Tori frowning. "Surely

that guy woke up by now. He bumped his head pretty hard, but he was only knocked out."

Amber sounds haunted. "If anything bad happens to him, it's our fault. We could have gotten him a doctor. We just came from the hospital."

"Some criminal mastermind you are," I snort. "You're cloned from Clara Barton."

"I wish," Amber shoots back.

"The story's not on the news because it's no big deal," I insist. "In the real world, some poor schnook probably brains himself every time the wind blows."

"Yeah, but this poor schnook works for a billionaire, who's also one of the most prominent people in town," Eli argues. "What affects Tamara Dunleavy is a big deal in Jackson Hole."

"Maybe he didn't tell the police about us because he doesn't remember," Tori puts in. "He took a pretty major wallop."

I have to laugh. "Even if the guy has total amnesia, don't you think his boss is going to notice she doesn't have a Bentley anymore?"

Tori is frowning again. "Why would Tamara Dunleavy want to hide the fact that her car's been stolen?"

"Isn't it obvious?" asks Amber. "We know too much

about her and Project Osiris. If we get arrested, we might blab."

"Big deal," I comment. "You blabbed to the cops in Denver and all they did was send you to a shrink."

"This is different," Eli says thoughtfully. "Amber was a random kid who came out of nowhere with a wild story. In this case, the cops would come after us, and we'd all be telling the same story. They may not believe us, but they'd definitely look into it."

"So she's writing off a quarter-million-dollar car?" I challenge.

"Unless," Tori muses, "she's got a way to find us anytime she wants."

"She's rich, not magic." I point out.

"That chauffeur was messing with our bags!" Eli exclaims urgently. "What if he put tracking devices in them? Then she could come after us with private detectives or hired criminals—"

"Or Purple People Eaters!" Amber adds. "We have to search the backpacks—now!"

We pull over to the shoulder, pop the trunk, and fall on our bags. I snatch up the sparkly princess loser-pack and dump out the contents. No homing devices, no computer chips, no microphones—no technology. What we find is money. There are five crisp hundred-dollar bills in the side pocket of each knapsack.

"All right," I say, clutching the cash. "I don't get it. Why would the old bat send her driver to sneak money into our bags?"

"I do," Tori puts in quietly. "She feels guilty. She's trying to help."

"We came to her for help," Eli argues. "She denied everything and sent us away."

Tori is patient. "She can't give us the kind of help we need—not without admitting her part in Project Osiris. But she didn't want to leave us lost and broke."

"She's a saint," Amber agrees. "Nothing like cash to say 'Don't go away mad; just go away.'" Contemptuously, she opens her hand and allows the five hundreds to flutter down to the soft shoulder.

The rest of us practically break our necks chasing down every single bill.

"You're twice as crazy as the Denver cops think you are!" I rasp. "You don't throw away five hundred bucks!"

"As if all the money in the world could ever make up for what Osiris did to us."

Eli tries reason. "If there's one thing we've learned about the outside world, it's that it runs on money. We're going to need this cash for food and gas and shelter."

"And more Band-Aids," Tori adds. "Malik's bleeding."

Malik's hand snaps to his neck. He examines the blood smear and blanches. "See what you did?" he rages to Amber. "I got injured running down the money you threw away!"

"That's not it," Tori informs him. "You've been bleeding for the past fifty miles."

"Why didn't anybody tell me?"

"We were afraid you'd pass out behind the wheel and kill us all," Eli replies honestly. "Seriously, Malik, it's fine. Your life's blood isn't draining away."

Classic Frieden. When it's somebody else's blood he's a hero.

"Sorry, you guys," says Amber. "I just hate the idea of being bought off, that's all."

"For a few hundred bucks, anyway," I agree. "She's actually kind of a cheapskate, when you think about it, considering she's got billions." That gives me a brainstorm. "I wonder how much it's worth to her to keep Osiris a secret. We could trade our silence for a big pile of money."

"I can hardly wait to find out who you're cloned from," Tori drawls.

I take it as a compliment even though she didn't mean it

that way. "Somebody loaded, that's for sure. Maybe that's why it's so natural for me to drive a car like this."

"Silence is the one thing we can't afford for *any* money," Amber says firmly. "We need to tell our story and get justice."

"You tried telling our story in Denver," I remind her. "It didn't turn out too well."

Eli nods. "We have to have proof before we can go public. That's why we needed Tamara Dunleavy to back up what we say."

"But she didn't back us up," counters Tori. "And she never will."

"You mean that's it?" I demand. "Without the old bag we can't ever prove who we are?"

Eli looks at each of us in turn. "There's one other place to find evidence about Project Osiris: The conference room of the Plastics Works—in Serenity."

I'm blown away. "Go back to Happy Valley?"

Tori looks thoughtful. "It's not impossible, you know. Before, we couldn't because of the invisible barrier. But now that we don't have those chips in our heads—"

"Yeah, fine, we could get into town without throwing up our guts while our heads explode. But why would we want to? We almost got killed getting *out* of Happy Valley!" My voice catches. "One of us did get killed."

Hector. I try not to lose it over what happened to the shrimp, because—well, that's the kind of thing Hector would do. But the truth is, I think about him all the time—at least when I'm not doing something else, like sliding down the bed of a dump truck into a wood chipper, or having a sophisticated piece of electronics cut out of my neck. Even when I'm cruising down a mountain road behind the wheel of a very choice automobile, part of me is imagining where Hector would be—probably sitting on the hump—if only he wasn't so worthless in a crisis, and if his best friend had looked out for him like he should have.

To tell you the truth, even the hump is pretty luxe in a Bentley.

"It's risky," Eli agrees, "but we don't have a choice. Project Osiris is so top secret that the only proof it ever existed is inside that factory."

"If our parents spot us, we're right back where we started," Amber points out. "We could be serving ourselves up to the Purple People Eaters on a silver platter."

"And don't forget there are cameras all over town," adds Tori. "We'll have to be really careful to avoid them."

"Good thing we know the place," says Eli. "We grew up inside their tiny perfect community. Our whole lives, we were their lab rats and their wind-up toys. It's time to take what we learned and use it against them."

14

TORI PRITEL

The scenery is totally breathtaking.

I thought Serenity was beautiful. But the ride out of Jackson Hole starts out gorgeous and only gets more dramatic and impressive the farther we drive into the Rockies.

Not that this is a sightseeing trip. (And just in case I forget that, there's Malik.)

"If you show me one more mountain, Torific, you're going out the window," he warns darkly.

"Shut up, Malik." Amber jumps to my defense. "We're stuck in this car for a long time. We might as well see something. It isn't going to make it any easier to sneak into Serenity if we're miserable for fourteen hours."

"Fourteen hours," moans Malik, fidgeting in the passenger seat. (Eli has taken over the wheel.)

"Our whole lives we were stuck in a town the size of a postage stamp," I add. "One of the reasons we got out was to experience the world. Well, this is it."

"Not too much going on," Malik observes. "It isn't exactly NYC."

"Are you kidding?" I exclaim. "That lake is as glassy as a mirror. Look at those wildflowers. Can you believe the colors?"

Malik buries his face in the side of the headrest. "You sure you got all that chip out of my skull, Laska? I think I'm going to throw up."

We monitored that Jackson Hole news channel until we lost the station a couple of hours back. No talk about police on the trail of a missing Bentley and runaway kids. Obviously, that doesn't mean it might not be happening, but it's starting to look like Tamara Dunleavy is loaning us her car on top of the money she donated to our cause. That doesn't excuse what she did, but just the thought that someone's trying to help us makes me feel a teeny bit less alone.

The roads are busier than Old County Six, which goes through Serenity, but compared to the traffic in and around Denver, it's pretty deserted out here. That's a good thing—every time another car goes by we sit taller in our seats in an attempt to appear older. We don't have to look like adults; we just have to pass for sixteen-plus. Luckily, people mind their own business, which is the total opposite of Serenity, where any newcomer instantly draws all eyes. Nobody thinks it's a big deal that we're in a quarter-million-dollar Bentley. (Or maybe they don't notice cars.)

The first city we come to is called Rock Springs, Wyoming. A week ago, it would have seemed huge to us, but now we can tell it's smaller than Pueblo and would fit inside a tiny corner of Denver. We're starving by this point, so we stop at McDonald's, the restaurant with the big yellow *M*. It's actually kind of exciting—we've all heard about it, but none of us have ever eaten at one.

"This is the greatest food I've ever tasted," Malik declares.

Amber glares at him. "They fry everything but the drinks. You can feel the grease in the air oozing in through your skin pores."

"Which is *awesome*," Malik finishes. He turns to Eli and me. "I'm going to get some more chow."

I'm astounded. "You had three Big Macs! You can't still be hungry!"

"Yeah, but I want to try one of those Happy Meals. You get this cool SpongeBob toy."

Amber manages to shame him out of the Happy Meal, but he won't leave until he tries out the PlayPlace with the little kids. It goes okay until he gets wedged in the tunnel slide, and we have to pry him free. By then, the manager is giving us dirty looks, which doesn't fit the low profile we're hoping to keep. Even Malik agrees it's a good time to move on.

When we come out to the parking lot, there are half a dozen teenagers draped over the Bentley. They peer beyond us, looking for the parent who's driving.

Their leader seems to be the guy who's stretched out across the hood for all the world like he's lying on a feather bed. He spots the keys in Eli's hand.

"Hey, kid. Where's your mommy?"

Malik frowns. "Where's yours?"

Amber steps forward. "When you disrespect people's property, you're really disrespecting yourself." It's a classic Serenity line, something we've been hearing our entire lives. Considering Amber's the angriest of all of us at our parents, it's amazing how quick she is to repeat some of the stuff they taught us.

The teenagers just laugh. The leader stands up on the hood and plants a muddy construction boot on the windshield, leaving an imprint of the sole. "Who am I disrespecting now?"

It's kind of a scary moment, and the scariest part is it's impossible to tell what these kids want. They don't seem to be criminals like we saw around the Denver bus station. And if they wanted to steal the Bentley, why would they wait around for us to come back?

"Get off our car," Amber says firmly.

"Who's going to make us, rich girl? You? Or are you going to call your rich daddy to come hit us with his big, fat wallet?"

Amber reaches out, grabs the leader's leg just above the boot and gives a mighty yank. He comes flying off the hood and lands in a heap on the pavement of the parking lot.

"Hey—" Another teen lunges forward and grasps a handful of Amber's sleeve.

He never gets to a second syllable. Malik's fist shoots out like a battering ram, catching the kid full in the nose.

They're all off the car now, closing on Malik. I snatch up a wire mesh trash can and drop it over the shortest one, covering him in garbage and pinning his arms. Malik has planted his feet and is standing his ground, raining punches on all comers. His accuracy is astonishing. He never seems to miss. Nothing we learned in Serenity could prepare us for a confrontation like this. It's awful, violent, ugly, but I can't look away.

The car starts up, pulling me back to reality. Eli's behind the wheel. He's got the right idea, of course. Our best move is to end this and get away from here. We want to learn about the outside world, but this is enough of a lesson for one day. (Actually, it looks like we've learned too much already, especially Malik.)

The teenagers finally back off, and we pile into the car. One of them throws a bottle at us as we peel out of the parking lot. It hits the pavement behind the Bentley and shatters.

"You're lucky I get bored easy!" Malik shouts back at them out his window.

"Everybody okay?" Eli manages in a shaky voice.

"Never better," chuckles Malik, sucking on a skinned knuckle. He seems to have found out something about himself that he never knew before. Maybe we all have.

"Your hand's bleeding," I inform him.

"Still worth it," Malik decides. "I never felt so alive. I can't believe that was my first fight. Just my luck to grow up in the one place where it never happens. It's like thirteen years wasted."

I sigh. "Well, you made up for lost time."

We haven't been back on the road very long when the all-too-familiar wail of a police siren reaches us.

Eli peers into the rearview mirror. "Uh-oh."

I turn to gaze out the back window. A squad car is following us, and gaining fast.

Sudden panic. "Do you think those teenagers called the cops on us?"

"On *us*?" Amber echoes. "All we did was stick up for ourselves. *We* should tell the cops about *them*."

"Except that the only thing *they'll* have to explain is why they're jerks." Why am I the only one who can see to plan a few moves ahead? "*We'll* have to explain what we're doing with Tamara Dunleavy's Bentley."

It's as if all the air has been sucked out of our car. We hold our breath as the cop closes the gap, flashers whirling. It's stunning how things can change in a heartbeat in the strange world outside Serenity. If this police officer pulls us over, he's going to get a lot more than parking lot brawlers. He'll get a car we can't possibly own, driven by kids too young to be driving. And when our descriptions reach the Denver police . . .

"Turn around!" Eli hisses. "Don't let the cop see us looking at him!"

It's good advice, but it's also agony to listen to the siren getting louder. Eli's checking the mirror every couple of seconds now. I can see a vein pulsing in his neck. The black-and-white must be right on our back bumper.

"We can outrun him," Malik says to Eli. "No way a cop car can keep up with a Bentley if we go flat out."

"But a cop can radio other cops," I argue. "We could end up with the whole police force after us."

"I'll take my chances with that over getting arrested right now," Malik counters.

A blurp from the siren makes us jump. The flashers light up the Bentley. The officer pulls right beside us.

"Go-o-o!" Malik urges.

But Eli maintains our speed. Maybe he's frozen that way. (I know I am.)

The squad car swerves ahead of us, accelerates, and stops an SUV about a quarter mile up. When we whiz by a few seconds later, the uniformed cop is writing the driver a ticket.

Give Eli all the credit. The speedometer needle doesn't budge. That's cool under fire.

We start breathing again.

15

ELI FRIEDEN

The Bentley's GPS thinks we should follow the interstate south through Denver.

Me? Not so much.

That navigation system is part of a full touch screen computer, with internet access. The next time Malik drives, I do a little web surfing. Denver PD has connected the house break-in in Mountain View with the four kids who escaped from the Medical Arts building. We're wanted for evading custody, breaking and entering, petty larceny, and grand theft auto. I'm not sure if that's for the Campanellas' Jeep Wrangler, the Purple People Eaters' SUV, or both. They can't know about the Bentley.

We're not exactly criminal masterminds yet, but it sure

looks like we're on our way, kind of Outlaws, version 2.0. It's more than enough to make us find a route south that doesn't pass through Denver.

Pretty soon we see why the GPS didn't want us to go this way. It's no wider than Old County Six, cutting straight through the Rockies via hairpin turns, blind curves, and endless switchbacks. Half the time, we're tracing along a high ledge, protected only by a railing that wouldn't stop a tumbleweed, much less a big sedan. Experienced drivers would be nervous; for a kid who taught himself on Xbox, it's terrifying. Plus you have to go so slow that every mile takes as long as five miles on the interstate.

We encounter very few other cars. When it gets dark, I take over the wheel from Malik again. Lucky me.

Towns are few and far between, and we almost run out of gas. The low fuel light is on when we happen on a shack with a gas pump. The attendant assures us that if we'd come ten minutes later, he would have been gone for the night. He says the next gas station is forty miles away. We would never have made it.

"Where are we going to sleep tonight?" Tori asks.

"We aren't," Malik replies gruffly. "You see any hotels around here?"

We've passed some clusters of ski cabins, boarded up for the off-season. That's about it.

"The more distance we put between ourselves and Jackson Hole, the safer we'll be," I argue. "You never know when Tamara Dunleavy is going to decide she wants her Bentley back."

So we load up on candy bars and cheese doodles and keep on going. It's almost midnight.

The girls fall asleep in the back around one and Malik is snoring by one thirty. That might be the most nerve-racking part—being the only one awake in the car, struggling not to let the comfortable leather seat carry me off to dreamland and the Bentley off a cliff. Eventually, the sound of me slapping myself in the face to stay alert disturbs Malik and we switch spots. We pass a road that claims to lead to Pueblo, so we know we're making progress. I think of Randy and wonder if his parents are mad at him for hiding us. It feels like a hundred years ago. I think of the Purple People Eaters we stranded there. I don't have to wonder if they're angry.

As morning approaches, the sky begins to lighten, but we see no sunrise. The mountains are in the way. And they're no longer the dramatic whites and grays of the high Rockies. They're lower, rounder, greener. They're *familiar.*

"I think we're getting close," I announce.

Sure enough, a few minutes later, we pass a sign:

WELCOME TO NEW MEXICO
LAND OF ENCHANTMENT

I don't know what it does for the others, but it makes the hair stand up on the back of my neck. For the clones of Project Osiris, there's nothing very homey about home. Returning to Serenity is less a sentimental journey, and more like sticking your head into the lion's mouth.

The navigation says we're forty-five miles away. Not from Serenity—there's no such destination on the Bentley's GPS. We're heading to Taos, the nearest town. From there, our plan is just to drive south until we hit Old County Six, which should take us right into town.

As we get closer to Taos, I feel an excitement building that has nothing to do with our mission. When you live in Serenity, almost everything from the outside world comes from Taos. All our clothes were bought there; our toys when we were little; our electronics and sports equipment when we got older. Tree trimmers, roofers, and driveway pavers—all Taos companies. They built our tree houses and set up our basketball hoops. Also plumbers, electricians, mechanics, repair people. When something breaks and Mr. Amani can't fix it, you call Taos. Twice a year, a visiting Taos dentist checked our teeth.

But in another way, Taos is as alien to us as Denver or Jackson Hole or the surface of the moon. None of us has ever seen it. So when we actually get there, we're amazed how small it is, even smaller than Jackson. It's the same kind of place, though, with lots of hotels, restaurants, and souvenir shops.

"*This* is Taos?" Malik exclaims.

"I pictured it different," murmurs Tori. "Bigger. Everything comes from here."

"What did we expect?" Amber muses. "A giant warehouse of refrigerators and TVs and a roomful of exterminators waiting for one of us to find a nest of rattlesnakes in the attic?"

"Well, no," Malik admits. "But I expected more than this. This is—nothing. Barely bigger than Happy Valley. And where is everybody?"

"Sleeping," Tori replies. "It's only five thirty."

Our plan is to sneak into Serenity, eighty miles away, under cover of darkness. If we show up in broad daylight, the Purples will spot us in a heartbeat. That means we've got a lot of hours to pass. A spirited debate is underway:

should we check into a motel here in Taos to catch up on our sleep, or is that too risky in a place that's so much a part of Project Osiris's orbit?

"Stop!" Tori shrieks suddenly.

Malik stomps on the brakes so hard that only our seatbelts keep us from going through the windshield.

"What?" I ask.

She points. Across the street, in front of a low-roofed industrial building, sits a faded blue panel truck. On the side, in chipped orange lettering, is painted:

SPLASH! POOL MAINTENANCE
TAOS, NM

We recognize it instantly. Serenity may be tiny, but every single house plus the school has a pool. Splash! serviced and supplied them all.

"Big deal," says Malik. "That truck was at my house almost as often as I was."

"Exactly!" Tori can barely get the words out fast enough. "That truck is as common around Serenity as the factory ones."

"So?"

"So if we drive it into town, nobody will look twice at it. Or at us."

It's a good idea—a great idea—but Amber pours cold water on it: "We don't have the keys."

"Cars get stolen all the time by guys who don't have the keys," Malik reasons. "There has to be a way."

I lean over and tap the Google icon on the Bentley's touch screen. "One thing about the real internet—you can learn how to do anything."

Before we know it, a new term has been added to our vocabulary:

Hot-wire.

16

MALIK BRUDER

Just because our lives are a lie, and the odds of us pulling off what we're trying to do are, like, a zillion to one, doesn't mean we can't have any fun.

Hot-wiring the truck, for instance.

Especially with Frieden pulling up instructions from the internet. Seriously, the guy could get anything from a computer. If we needed to sprout wings and fly to Happy Valley, Eli could pull up a list of the top ten places to buy feathers.

Then there's Laska, who takes all the information and organizes it like it's one of her lists. I can almost picture this one: THINGS TO DO TODAY (TRUCK-STEALING EDITION).

It's 5:42, but Taos is still asleep and deserted—at least

in the area where Splash! is located. It's all businesses around here—no houses. Which is a good thing because Eli is making a racket whacking away at the padlock on the back of the truck with a rock.

I hold out my hand. "Let me try."

"The metal's too strong," he says in consternation.

"Give it to me."

I take the rock, walk around to the side of the truck, and bash a hole in the window. I clear away the sharp shards, reach in, and open the door.

The other three are staring at me in horror.

"What?" I ask. "Like stealing a truck is okay, but you can't break the window that's attached to it?"

To their credit, they keep their mouths shut. We know that we have to do some bad stuff, but it's hard to get past all that honesty, harmony, and contentment that's been shoved down our throats. It looks like I'm getting there before the others.

I crawl into the space between the front seats and look around. The back of the truck is filled with hoses and nets and jugs of pool chemicals. There's a giant industrial-power vacuum, and—my eyes fall on the toolbox. I open it. It has everything you could possibly need for installing and repairing pool heaters. And hot-wiring a truck.

I take out what we need—screwdriver, wire-cutters, electrical tape, and rubber gloves. It's funny: this should be the hardest thing in the world, but the instructions Eli gets make it as simple as putting together one of those Lego models Hector used to build. Poor Hector—he would have been better at this than me. He was better at most things—except keeping himself alive.

I use the screwdriver to pry at the cover of the steering column, and am surprised at how easily it pops off. The gloves are next—can't risk a shock when messing with electricity. Basically, you just have to find the red power wires and the brown starter wires, rip them out of the ignition, strip the ends, and connect them directly. Once the power is hooked up, the instant I touch the frayed ends of the starter wires, the pool truck roars to life.

It's one of the most satisfying sounds I've ever heard.

I smirk at them though the hole in the broken window. "Last call for the Happy Valley Express. You snooze, you lose. Have your tickets ready."

The girls climb into the back, making themselves as comfortable as possible amid the buckets and bug-dippers.

Eli holds back. "What about the Bentley?"

I shrug. "Who needs a quarter-million-dollar classic

when you've got a rickety piece of junk like this?"

"Think," Eli persists. "If a car registered to a famous billionaire is found abandoned in Taos, it's going to make the papers. My dad calls his old partner, and she tells him we stole her car. He'll know we're headed back to Serenity, and I don't want him rolling out the welcome wagon."

"We could drive it into the river," Amber suggests.

I'm sure I turn pale. "Don't wreck it. It's just so awesome."

"If it gets us caught," she returns, "it's not awesome. It's a liability."

"It doesn't have to disappear forever," Tori reasons. "We just need the time to sneak into Serenity, get what we need, and sneak back out again."

We make an interesting parade around the quiet streets of Taos—a billionaire's limo followed by a rusty old pool truck. We finally find a small storm-shuttered ski chalet flying a tattered Chicago Bears flag, and leave the Bentley behind the house, out of view of the road. With any luck, these Bears fans won't find it until they come back during ski season, several months away.

Eli leaves a note on the dashboard—like that makes everything okay:

Sorry, Ms. Dunleavy, but if you won't help us, we have to help ourselves.

I nod wisely. "Like, for instance, we helped ourselves to her car."

"Just because we're cloned from crooks doesn't mean we have to act like them," he lectures.

We jump into the truck, and we're finally on our way. 6:10.

Happy Valley or bust.

When the road out of Taos comes to Old County Six, the shudder that goes through the four of us shakes the rickety old truck. We're feeling everything all at once: triumph that we've found it; relief that this un-place we come from isn't a figment of our imaginations; and plain fear that we're putting our hard-won freedom at risk by going back there.

We've been on a lot of lonely, lousy roads but Old County Six beats them all hands down. Remember, the aim of Project Osiris was to put their clone farm in an out-of-the-way place, and they really hit the jackpot on that score. The Splash! truck bounces and rattles over every bump and rut.

The ride is misery, but we wish it was a whole lot longer,

knowing what comes at the end of it. There are no signs telling us how far away Serenity is, but we've been in the truck at least an hour and a half, so we know we must be close.

"Look!" Eli is white as a ghost.

Up ahead, the road curves sharply, and a large section of railing has been torn away. It can only be the place where the cone truck went flying over the side into the valley below.

I stop and nobody needs to ask why. Amber and Tori crawl up from the back to peer out the window. It's the first definite sign of Serenity, but it's much more than that. This is the place Hector died.

I don't cry, or barf, or lose control of the truck, or anything like that. But I wasn't sure until this minute that I wasn't going to.

Tori is the first to speak. "This spot should be in the middle of the invisible barrier, and we're all okay."

Eli nods. "We were right about those chips in our necks. That's what was making us get sick."

"It also means we're almost there," I add.

Eli climbs into the back with the girls, and Tori hands me a baseball cap and cheap sunglasses.

I'm the pool guy who's there nearly every day. Nobody's going to notice me.

I put the truck in gear, and we climb the next rise. Suddenly, there it is—not just a glimpse of it, but the whole town. Serenity, New Mexico, from the smokestacks of the Plastics Works to the perfect houses with their perfect pools.

It always looked dinky to me; it looks dinkier now. The entire street grid would fit easily inside the little Denver neighborhood where the Campanellas live. A pimple on the landscape. Home sweet home.

For nearly fourteen years, this was my entire universe. I hated it, not only for its dinkiness, but also for the wider world it was keeping me from. Of course, that wasn't half as much as I hated it when I learned about Project Osiris.

And now I hate it for something new—the stomach-churning dread I feel as we roll toward it.

The clock tower issues a single chime, signifying eight thirty a.m.

"School must be starting," says Amber, whose mother was our teacher.

"My parents are just getting to the factory," adds Tori in a trembling voice.

We're all thinking about our families, and the fact that we're as physically close to them as we've been since we took off on Serenity Day. It's impossible not to blame them for what they did to us, but they're the nearest thing to parents we're ever going to have. Here we are, hiding in our pool truck, when our gut impulse is run home and hug them. Or in Eli's case, shake hands with his dad.

Or maybe not. A glance over my shoulder reveals that Eli is the only one of us who is stone-faced and cold.

I picture my own father with his goofy bow tie, opening his little clinic, wondering if anyone's going to be sick today, providing an audience for his corny jokes. And my mother, the ballet instructor, who lost her one and only student when Laska blew out of town. She's probably been using the extra time to work on her cooking, which was pretty awesome to begin with. I haven't had a decent meal since—except maybe McDonald's.

I pass the sign at the city limits.

WELCOME TO SERENITY
AMERICA'S IDEAL COMMUNITY

"Ideal," I mutter. "Yeah, right. Ideal for clones—until they figure out what's going on and blow this Popsicle stand."

"What do you see?" Tori urges. With the three of them in the back of the windowless truck, I'm the only one with a view of the town.

"Nothing," I reply. "It's Happy Valley. What's to see?"

The fact is, though, I'm practically blown away by how *nice* everything is. I never noticed it when I lived here, since I had nothing to compare it to. But now that I've lived in the outside world, I can appreciate how flawless this place is. Old County Six is suddenly smooth as glass. And when I turn onto Harmony Street, all the houses look like they were painted yesterday, without a single untrimmed bush or a blade of grass out of place. The basketball hoops stand ramrod-straight, their posts perpendicular to the driveways.

When I see Hector's house, I have to fight down an impulse to run in there and apologize to his parents for not looking after him well enough. Then again, Hector got the worst parents of any of us, so they probably don't even care.

Next comes my own house, three driveways down. The door is open at least three inches, and I know Mom's not going to be happy about that. One of her favorite lectures is "We're not paying to air-condition the entire state of New Mexico . . ." Dad's going to catch some flak over this.

I give them a mumbled play-by-play. "There's your place, Frieden . . . and yours, Torific. You left the light on in your studio in the attic . . . hey, Laska, did I ever tell you your curtains are ugly?"

"Is there anybody out there?" Tori asks eagerly.

"No one."

That's when it dawns on me. I haven't seen a single human being so far. No one watering flowers or pushing a baby carriage or even a hint of movement through a window. At the park, I gaze beyond the Serenity Cup in its Plexiglas case to the kids' playground. Not a soul.

I turn to face the others. "There's nobody here."

"They're all at school or at work," Eli reasons.

"You don't get it," I persist. "It's a ghost town—I mean more than the usual level of nothing. And the cars seem to be gone too."

We try the school, which should be a busy place this time of day. Silent, dark, and empty. Ditto the general store and restaurant, the town hall, and my dad's clinic.

"I was right!" Amber exclaims. "Project Osiris is so evil that our parents couldn't risk getting caught. When the Purple People Eaters couldn't capture us, they had to shut down the whole experiment and disappear."

"Or," Eli adds in a worried tone, "this is a trap, and that's exactly what they want us to think."

"If that was true," Tori reasons, "we'd be surrounded by Purples right now."

"Unless they're hiding somewhere, waiting for us to get

out of the truck," I add nervously. That would be just like our loving families. Home is where the double cross is.

It's an anxious moment. We're all pretty sure there's nobody around. But if we're stepping into their trap, that's a move we can't take back. In the end, there's only one way to find out for sure. We have to go to the Plastics Works.

The plant is on the "far" edge of town. But remember: nothing can be considered very far in this pimple on the hairy butt of the southwest, where an eight-minute walk gets you from one side to the other. I ride the brakes down the Fellowship hill, feeling my stomach begin to clench. The Plastics Works is Purple People Eater territory, and our pool service cover won't hold up in an area where there are no houses or pools. If we're going to run into trouble, it'll be here.

I stop at the gate we used to use to sneak onto factory property. The two remaining cone trucks are parked on the other side of the fence. No people, purple or otherwise.

"Try the front entrance," Eli suggests.

I hesitate. "What if the whole town is gathered on the steps, arguing over what to do about us?"

"Then be ready to stomp on the gas and get us out of there," Tori supplies.

"Are you kidding? This bucket of bolts couldn't outrun

a tricycle. Now, if we had my Bentley—"

"We don't," Amber says impatiently. "Just do it."

If this hunk of junk had a decent muffler, we'd be able to hear our hearts pounding as we round the corner to the main entrance.

Nothing. No parents. No Purples. No sign of life at all.

17

ELI FRIEDEN

It's too weird. How come Serenity is deserted?

Tori's nervousness bubbles over. "Where is everybody?"

"You'd prefer a platoon of Purples surrounding the truck?" inquires Malik.

I think it over. "Just because there's no one around doesn't mean the factory's empty. Remember, Osiris headquarters is in there, and also the desk where they monitor all the security cameras around town."

We park the truck behind a tall stand of sagebrush, disconnecting the power and starter wires to turn off the motor. We're now totally exposed. If this *is* a trap, we're done.

Lead in our feet, we straggle across the road toward the factory entrance. This is uncharted territory. The Plastics Works is off-limits to nonemployees. There are never any holiday parties, open houses, or take-your-kid-to-work days. The one time we did go inside, we scaled the back wall, climbed up on the roof, and entered through the air-conditioning vent.

But here it is, a glassed-in entrance under the big sign: *Serenity Plastics Works.* There's no one at the reception desk. I look down and see a pathetic bundle of feathers lying on the front steps. By its crest and its coloring, I know it's a mountain blue jay—they're common in Serenity. Flies buzz around the body, so it's been dead a while.

Tori notices it too. "It must have crashed into the glass and broken its neck. Poor thing."

"Doesn't seem very Serenity," Malik comments. "You know, having to wade through bird guts just to get to their precious factory."

Amber makes a face. "Does everything have to be gross with you?"

"I'm making a point," he says patiently. "You know this town—you drop a gum wrapper and someone's got it in a trash can before it even hits the ground. If there are dead birds around the Plastics Works, it takes the happy out of Happy Valley. It means there's nobody home."

I'm wondering how to get inside, yet the minute I step in front of the door, it slides open. We look at each other—this seems too easy. Still, there's nothing to do but walk right in.

The acrid smell hits us almost immediately. Smoke—not dense, billowing clouds, but a light gray haze in the air.

"Where there's smoke there's fire," says Amber.

"Or there *was*," Tori amends. "I don't think anything's burning now."

Malik throws open a massive steel door that leads to the vast plant floor. Tori and I have seen it once before, from a ventilation grate about forty feet up. The point of view is different, yet the reality is the same: no machinery, no raw materials, just a few hundred orange traffic cones in case they have to pretend that this is a real operation and they're making something here. Besides that, a forklift, a riding lawnmower, a few random pieces of furniture and shelving. That's it.

"So this is what an un-factory looks like," Malik observes.

"My dad spent every day in this place!" Amber says bitterly. "He worked *overtime*! He complained about shipping problems, and rush orders that needed filling!"

The rest of us nod. Even when we know the truth, it's jarring to see Serenity's pride and joy laid bare as an empty shell.

Tori sighs. "No smoke in here, anyway."

It occurs to the four of us at the same time. The conference room! Our evidence!

The realization jolts us into sudden, frantic action, but the truth is we don't know how to find the room we're looking for. We've been there before via the roof, not the main entrance.

We scramble around throwing open doors, revealing mostly bathrooms and storage closets. That's when I remember—there was definitely a door from the conference room leading directly onto the factory floor.

We snake our way through the stacked cones to the only exit on the north side. Malik throws the door wide and stale smoke comes billowing out. We pull our collars up over our noses and run inside, waving our arms to try to disperse the clouds. I jam a traffic cone under the door to keep it propped open.

As the smoke escapes into the soaring factory space, shapes become more distinct and we get our first glimpse of the wreckage of Osiris headquarters.

"Look what they've done," Amber chokes. "Those evil, rotten—"

"They cloned criminals, Laska," Malik growls. "What's worse than that? Torching the evidence is nothing in comparison."

The whiteboards that had documented the lives of eleven clones, complete with pictures and notes, are nothing but a pile of ash. The heat of the fire melted the glass of the table, which sags in the middle, forming what looks like a giant fruit bowl. Metal filing cabinets are blackened and crumpled like juice boxes. I open one and find its handle still a little warm to the touch. Its contents are dust that flies into my face, making me cough.

"Our evidence!" Tori exclaims in agony. "Now we'll never be able to prove what's been done to us!"

I get down on my hands and knees and start sifting through the mess, heedless of the fact that gray grit is beginning to cover me from head to toe. It's everywhere, stinging my eyes, up my nose, even in my mouth, and I spit ash that reminds me of burnt toast.

"You're wasting your time, Frieden," Malik groans. "There's nothing left bigger than a postage stamp. Your dad sure knows how to cover his tracks."

"Why is it only my dad?" Maybe it's because our one chance has literally gone up in smoke, but this really gets to me. "Your parents were in it up to their necks! Everybody's were!"

Malik doesn't back down. "Yeah, but it takes a special kind of sicko to dream up Project Osiris! None of our folks did that. Just Felix Frieden—or should I say Hammerstrom?"

"Look"—Tori steps between us—"we're all upset—"

I barely hear her. "First off, my father didn't invent Osiris on his own. Tamara Dunleavy was with him at the beginning. And second, who started it isn't as important as who *did* it, and that was every adult in town!"

"At least my dad's a doctor!" he returns. "He *helps* people!"

"By filling them full of pills to make them forget the truth of this place!"

Malik towers menacingly over me. "On whose orders? Your old man's, that's who!"

"Guys—" Tori pleads.

"My old man's a scientist!" I sputter. "This began as an experiment—" I can't believe I'm defending Felix Frieden, who has to be every bit as bad as the criminals he cloned to create us. But I'm too mad to back down. I get right in Malik's face. For a second, I'm pretty sure I'm about to get punched out by the guy who took down a gang of teenagers in a McDonald's parking lot. He's even got his fists up, ready to let fly. I can practically taste the blood mingling with the smoke and ash.

At the last second, Malik transfers his rage from me to a

vase lying broken between us on the floor. He rears back his foot and kicks it across the room. The pieces go flying in all directions, along with the stems of dead flowers.

We see it at the same time—a single sheet of paper, singed at the edges. I bend down and pick it up, cradling it in my hands.

"How did it survive the fire?" Malik asks, his anger turning to wonder.

The page is damp, the ink blotchy and running. "The vase must have fallen on it when they were torching the place. And the water from the flowers kept it from burning up."

"It's the only thing left," Amber mourns. "And it's ruined."

"For all we know, it's somebody's laundry list, anyway," Malik puts in sadly. "If you see anything about bow ties, that's my dad. As if a dumb bow tie makes you any less a sicko," he adds with a sheepish look at me.

"Yeah, I'm sorry too," I tell him.

Amber peers at the soggy paper. "It *is* a list, you know. You can tell by the way the ink blotches are spaced."

"Who cares?" Malik laments. "We'll never be able to read it. We came all this way, and for what? Happy Valley wins. We may be the masterminds, but they're the ones who are always a step ahead."

Tori is wearing a look that I've learned to recognize—the one where she's concentrating so hard you should be able to hear the gears turning. "The freezer!" she exclaims suddenly.

We stare at her.

"It's an old artist's trick," she explains. "If you spill something on a painting, you put it in a deep freeze. It stops the water from soaking into the paper and solidifies the picture. If we can freeze-dry the moisture out of this, maybe it'll reveal what's there."

"But where are we going to find a freezer in a plastics factory?" asks Malik.

Amber laughs in his face. "We're in Serenity, dummy, and we've got the whole town to ourselves. Pick a house, any house."

18

TORI PRITEL

Home.

I never thought I'd see it again. And now that I'm here, I feel like an intruder, a burglar. (Which I technically am, I guess.)

In all the time I lived in Serenity, my parents never locked our front door even once. But now that they're abandoning ship, they sealed the house up tight. It's almost like a message to me: *Keep out. You don't live here anymore.*

Obviously, I realize I *escaped* from this place. Nobody banished me. Still, the idea that I'm a trespasser in the Pritel home—*my* home—makes me really, really sad.

We have to break in through the stained-glass panel in the door—the one Mom and Dad said they were so proud of. I made it for their fifteenth anniversary. It took me almost a month; it takes Malik half a second to put the pointed hat of a garden gnome through it. It's a lot easier to destroy things than to create them. As an artist, I've always been on the "create" side, but I can't help but appreciate the speed and directness of Team Destruction. After all, Project Osiris was more than fourteen years in the making, and we busted it up in a single wild night.

We chose my house because of my studio in the attic. If we're going to have any chance of bringing out what it says on the mysterious list from the Plastics Works, this is obviously the place to be. I have gallery lighting, not to mention magnifying lamps with special viewing lenses. If that won't do it, nothing will. One thing about living in an experiment—there was always plenty of money for the very best stuff.

Right now, though, the paper is in our Sub-Zero freezer, next to Steve's (my dad's) favorite steaks, and our homemade ice pops in the shape of the Serenity Cup. We used to eat them on our porch after the fireworks on Serenity Day. That didn't happen this year, for obvious reasons. I wonder why my parents didn't throw them out. Maybe they were secretly hoping I'd change my mind and come home. I have to admit I still long for that front porch and the comfort of their company and knowing I'm part of a family. At this point, though, that wouldn't mean much. A Popsicle is just a piece of ice, and my only blood relative is behind bars somewhere, serving a well-deserved prison term.

The Sub-Zero freezer is turned to the coldest possible setting. While we wait for the paper to chill out, we raid our former houses in search of clothes that fit us better than the stuff we took from the Campanellas. Mr. Campanella's jeans have been hanging lower and lower on Malik's waist as life on the run stretches them out, and he's beyond psyched to ditch the princess backpack for a normal black one. I know Amber is anxious to get into a T-shirt that fits. She's so nuts about her goal weight that any tightness is like an alarm bell in her head. Me, I'm just thrilled to jettison the pink and sequins. Way too flashy.

My clothes are here, but—am I crazy, or is everything in the wrong place? I check all the drawers with the same result. Nothing is missing, but the contents have been slightly rearranged. I experience a chill as I picture my parents going through all my stuff, looking for clues to where we might be.

They love me; they love me not. (Or at least their loyalty to Project Osiris comes first.)

Upstairs in the attic studio, there's evidence of the same kind of search, only here, something really *is* missing—the photographs we snapped of the eleven whiteboards from the conference room.

I tell the others when we gather back at my house. They confirm that their rooms have been ransacked too, although nothing seems to have been taken except my box of pictures.

Amber is alarmed. "Those pictures were proof of Project Osiris!"

Eli thinks it over. "Not really. I mean, you could make out the names and see the pictures, I guess. But the writing was too small to read. I don't think there was any hard evidence we could take to the police."

"And even if we tried, our parents could just deny it," Malik adds. "You know, say we made the boards ourselves."

He's right. We haven't lost anything that would do us any good.

We're all pretty hungry, so I boil hot dogs and open a couple of tins of soup—the extent of my talents as a chef.

Malik makes fun of me when he sees me loading the dishwasher. "Who's going to know?"

"*I'll* know," I reply, tight-lipped.

Malik sets a pastry box down on the table. "My mom's peanut butter cookies. They have to be a little stale, but that's still better than what anyone else bakes." You can hear the nostalgia in his tone. "Hector used to inhale these things. Too bad the shrimp can't be here to hog the whole batch."

That's our lunch: hot dogs with bread instead of buns, vegetable soup, Hector's favorite cookies, and Serenity Cup ice pops. The milk has gone sour, so we drink water.

Eli's brought his iPad and we amuse ourselves by looking stuff up on Serenity's fake internet. It's hard not to laugh while he quotes endless statistics on how many hundreds of thousands of traffic cones the Plastics Works churned out last month, or reads the highlights of President Roosevelt's speech at the founding of Serenity in 1937 (which never happened, since there never was a town here until Project Osiris created it in 1999). He passes the tablet on to Malik, who finds extensive sports coverage of water polo matches all around the country, with no mention of football, baseball, basketball, or hockey, which Serenity considers too competitive and violent. When it's my turn, I list all the awards our town has supposedly won over the years—America's Ideal Community, Best Quality of Life, Top Schools, Lowest Unemployment, Safest City, Purest Air Quality, and on and on. By the time I get to Least Traffic Congestion, the others are rolling on the floor. Traffic—in a place with hardly any cars and not so much as a single stoplight!

It's awful, but it feels good to laugh. I almost forgot what that's like. And maybe the fact that we *can* laugh means there's hope for us. We aren't the people they told us we were, but this could be a glimpse of the people we'll one day be. If we can think for ourselves, and learn, and even have a little fun occasionally, there's a chance that we can leave the past behind. We *are* Project Osiris, but Project Osiris isn't all we are.

There's an expression we've heard in the outside world: "Get a life." That's what we have to do.

Malik shakes his head. "All those brilliant scientists, and not one of them figured out that we were going to get older and start to question the load of baloney they were feeding us."

Amber takes the tablet next, accesses the online dictionary, and looks up *clone*.

ENTRY NOT FOUND.

"There's a word we weren't allowed to learn," she drawls, deadpan. "I wonder why?"

For some reason, the whole thing isn't very funny anymore. There were a lot of words we weren't supposed to know—*murder*, for example. But the fact that the name of the very thing we are was forbidden to us—well, that says a lot about our lives.

Eli fidgets uncomfortably in his chair. "You think that paper's frozen enough yet?"

We're all glad to change the subject.

I open the freezer door and take out the large Ziploc bag. The plastic is fogged up, which I know is a good sign. That means the moisture has come off the page.

We gather around the table as I open the zipper and gingerly draw the paper out.

The ink is still mottled, but the blotches have shrunk to the point where definite letters are now visible. It's not readable, exactly. Yet if we look at it under different light, and go word by word . . .

"Follow me!" I exclaim, and lead the way up the stairs to the attic. In my studio, I clip the document onto my drafting desk, swivel the magnifying lamp over it, and peer through the lens.

It's the same mess, only larger and brighter. But with my artist's eye, I can envision the lines as they were being formed, and painstakingly put it together, letter by letter.

The others are crowded so closely behind me that the combined effect of their breathing on the back of my neck sends shivers clear down to my heels. I shoo them away and return my attention to the list.

And it *is* a list. A list of names. The first couple of lines are smeared beyond reading, but I can make out a lot of the rest of it:

Gus Alabaster
Brother Juan Antonio Lanterna
Archibald Barrett, MD
Mickey Seven
Q. Sinjin Lee . . .

The wet page might have creased here, because the next line is just a smudge. But I'm able to make out the rest of the list:

Yvonne-Marie Delacroix
Farouk al Fayed
C. J. Rackoff

Without looking away from the magnifying lamp, I pull over a notebook and scribble down everything I've managed to pull off the paper.

Malik frowns over my shoulder. "That's it? A bunch of strangers?"

"Just because we don't recognize the names doesn't mean they aren't important," I tell him. "Otherwise they wouldn't be here."

"Maybe they're the Purple People Eaters," Amber suggests. "They aren't really named things like Rump L. Stiltskin and Baron Vladimir von Horseteeth."

Malik shakes his head. "No way. There are no female Purples, and there are at least three girls on this list."

"These could be our parents," I suggest. "We already know at least their last names are fake."

Eli has another theory. "We have seven names, but there are four more that we can't read. That adds up to eleven, which is a very familiar number. Eleven of us—eleven clones."

The earth stands still as we digest this. When we learned about Project Osiris, we lost our sense of where we came from. Not from our parents; not from *any* parents. We were left with a murky idea of a splotch of DNA from an anonymous criminal rotting in an anonymous prison somewhere over the rainbow.

But—my heart begins to beat double-speed—these are real names. Real people . . .

Malik is amazed. "Are you saying that's—*us*?"

Amber clues in. "Not us. The people we're cloned from.

Like Bartholomew Glen."

"He's not on the list," I observe.

"I'll bet he is," says Eli, looking unhappy. "He must be one of the smudges."

Poor Eli. I think he believes he's the one cloned from the Crossword Killer. I guess it's possible, but Eli Frieden is not the murderer type. He's sensitive and gentle and smart. I'd never say it out loud, but I'm kind of leaning toward Malik for Bartholomew Glen—except that, for a tough guy, he practically faints when you serve him a medium rare hamburger. And anyway, isn't the whole point of Osiris to prove that we're not destined to be exactly the same as the people we're cloned from?

Malik has a practical question. "How are we going to find out?"

"The same way we did with Glen," Eli reasons. "As soon as we connected a name from the factory with a criminal mastermind, we knew we had a DNA donor. If these seven turn out to be criminals . . ."

I swallow hard. I'm not sure I want to know.

No, scratch that. I obviously do. But I'm terrified of what I'm about to find out.

19

AMBER LASKA

GUS ALABASTER (1948–) is a powerful organized crime figure who ran west and northwest Chicago for twenty-two years before his arrest in 2001 on federal tax evasion charges. His control over O'Hare airport gave him national and international reach. Considered by the FBI to be "the most successful gangster in American history," Alabaster was almost as accomplished as a media darling as he was as a mobster . . .

We're back at the factory, where we can rely on the internet being the real thing. At Tori's house, there was no such person as Gus Alabaster when we researched him on Eli's iPad. But here—not in the burnt-out conference room, but in the offices above it—the name alone generates over 200,000 hits.

This is my first time here—I was late to the plan to escape Serenity. Don't think I'm not ashamed of that. I used to be this awful place's biggest fan. If not for the others, I never would have seen past the honesty, harmony, and contentment. I was too busy thanking my lucky stars for being born in this wonderful community.

. . . Alabaster was often seen in the company of celebrities, sports heroes, fashion models, political figures, and even royalty, chauffeured around Chicago in his signature white Rolls Royce.

Federal, state, and local police charged Alabaster with 147 counts of crimes ranging from armed robbery to racketeering to conspiracy to commit murder. The nimble gangster was cleared every time, which only added to his legend. In the end, though, tax evasion proved to be the charge Alabaster could not beat. The swashbuckling mob boss could not explain how someone who did not earn enough to pay any income tax could own six houses, fourteen cars, two yachts, and a private jet . . .

We gather around the iPad. There's a picture of the smiling mob boss in a nightclub, surrounded by Las Vegas showgirls, and another of him lighting up a big, fat cigar directly in front of a *No Smoking* sign. He's grinning even wider in a photo from his 2001 trial, and in the shot from his first day in prison, he's practically beaming. The guy must be crazy. The worse his life goes, the bigger the smile on his face. It's not happiness, of course; it's defiance. He's showing the world that no matter what happens, it doesn't bother him in the slightest.

Eli scrolls down to the final picture on the web page. It's a black-and-white close-up image of a teenage Gus Alabaster with a black eye and a crooked smirk. The caption reads: *Mug shot from first arrest, age 15.*

Four identical gasps threaten to suck all the air out of the room. I've seen this face before. I'm looking at it now, hanging over my left shoulder.

It's Malik.

Eli, Tori, and I take a step backward. I've had my problems with Malik, but I feel so awful for him. How will he react to learning that he's cloned from this despicable gangster?

"I knew it!" Malik cackles gleefully. "I just knew my guy would turn out to be somebody cool!"

We stare at him. "Cool?" I echo. "He's a ruthless criminal who's spending the rest of his life behind bars!"

Malik is undaunted. "But when he was out he had six houses, fourteen cars, two yachts, and a private jet!"

"According to this, the government took a lot of it away," Eli reminds him.

"The government," Malik snorts. "Who listens to them? We're living proof of that. They said no cloning. And what did they get? Cloning. Anyway, gangster's not so bad. It's way better than that Bartholomew Crossword guy. At least he's not a serial killer."

"Only because he had hired guns to do his killing for him," I put in.

Eli studies his sneakers, waiting for his own identity, and nervous it might come up Bartholomew Glen. At least we girls have been spared that possibility.

Tori sighs. "Let's just move on. I kind of doubt this is the biggest shock we're going to get today."

Brother Juan Antonio Lanterna turns out to be a monk who was arrested for running a major counterfeiting operation in the cellar of his monastery. He died in prison in 2010. There's no picture of him as a kid, but his intense burning eyes and long pointy nose look a lot like Robbie Miers.

"He's one of us," Tori confirms, as if we need reminding. None of us will ever forget the names on the eleven whiteboards—the eleven Osiris clones.

Eli pounds the tablet's virtual keyboard. "Miers is *peace*

in Latvian." All our fake last names mean things like peace, love, and brotherhood in other languages.

"Robbie." I let my breath out and realize I've been holding it. We weren't friends, exactly. Still, when you grow up with only twenty-nine other kids, everybody is kind of close. Robbie's quiet, a little on the shy side.

"Go, Robbie," Malik says with a laugh. "He's the last person I'd ever expect to be printing funny money—"

"*He* didn't," Eli interrupts him. "The guy he's cloned from did that."

"I wonder what happened to him and the others when our parents shut down Osiris and took off," I muse.

Nobody has an answer for that. We don't know—and have no way to know—what's been done with our fellow clones.

Archibald Barrett is a doctor who went to jail for trafficking in human organs for transplants. Eli is able to track down his high school graduation picture online. He looks exactly like Ben Stastny. Stastny—Czech for *contentment*. Chock up another one on our happy list. Poor Ben.

Next is Mickey Seven. She had this long Russian name, but people started calling her Seven because she was the seventh person busted in a march on the Virginia State Capitol protesting cuts to homeless shelters. According to the internet, she spent her whole life protesting something, and the older she got, the more violent her activism became. She was arrested sixteen times over the next eight years, serving several short prison sentences. In 1991, while protesting the First Gulf War, she led a group that blew up the armory at Brannigan Naval Base. She was declared a terrorist and sent to prison. Even in jail, she still spends most of her time riling up the other inmates to riot against the guards. The woman is a toxic mixture of anger, muleheadedness, and zero fear. She has absolutely no conscience. No wonder the courts extended her sentence to life. The last thing anyone would want is a rabble-rouser like that loose on the streets.

The web page has a reproduction of a newspaper article of her first arrest. I take in the picture. The Plastics Works tilts and I almost crumple to the floor.

I'm looking in a mirror.

In the photograph, Mickey Seven is older than I am—probably about eighteen. But there's no question that her face is my own. In the image, she's in the process of ripping a riot shield away from a cop and hitting him over the head with it. It's an action shot—her blond hair is flying; her eyes are ferocious. That's the part I recognize even more than her appearance—her intensity, her 100-percent confidence that she's doing the right thing.

I've felt like that, and I remember exactly when. It was the day I learned about Project Osiris and how my entire life was a lie. At that awful moment, I'm sure I looked just like the wild animal in the photograph.

Malik beams at me. "Welcome to the club, Laska. You might even be worse than me."

"Shut up," I mutter, but I'm too deflated to manage any volume. I wanted to know who I am. And now that I do, I wish I didn't.

Tori puts a sympathetic arm around my shoulders. "Sorry, Amber."

I bristle. "Don't 'sorry' me! There's nothing to be sorry about! I'm not this person. From now on, I'm going to do everything opposite from the way Mickey Seven would do it!"

Malik nods in amusement. "That's probably what Mickey Seven would say."

My eyes are slits. "Just wait and see."

We move on. Q. Sinjin Lee has to be the DNA donor for Aldwin Wo. *Wo*—a Chinese word for *peace*. It's hard to imagine him as an exact copy of the guy who ran one of the largest smuggling operations in American history. By the time the government added up all the charges against Lee, he was sentenced to over three hundred years behind bars. Not that he got to serve much of it. He was stabbed to death by another inmate last year.

We finally get to Tori when we research Yvonne-Marie Delacroix. There's no mistaking it. The website actually has a middle-school graduation picture. I've had sleepovers with the girl in that photo. We kept drawers of clothes at each other's houses. I called her parents pseudo-Mom and pseudo-Dad. The two are identical.

Everyone sees it except Tori herself. "It's impossible," she says firmly. "Yvonne-Marie Delacroix is a bank robber! I won four honesty badges last year!"

Eli tries to explain. "She's not just a bank robber. She's a genius at getting in and out of places. Doesn't that sound kind of familiar? Who got us into the Plastics Works that first time? You. Who got us out of the Medical Arts building? Who broke into the Campanellas' house?"

"But I didn't steal anything!"

"Not if you don't count clothes, food, backpacks, and a Jeep Wrangler," Malik agrees.

"I didn't steal that! I just rode in it!"

"Calm down," I urge. "Yes, we've done some bad things. It was the only way to survive."

"Right!" Tori clings to that. "I stole because I had no

choice! Yvonne-Marie Delacroix did it for the money!"

"And she was pretty good at it too," Malik reads on. "She was at her villa in Tuscany by the time Interpol caught up with her. Her 1985 Fort Knox robbery is still a required class in FBI training."

"I don't want to be a required class in FBI training!" Tori wails.

I put a sympathetic arm around her shoulders. It was hard enough learning we were exact copies of terrible criminals. But that doesn't compare to the horror of finding out which ones—to seeing that picture of someone who's you, and yet not you, along with details of the awful crimes this person has committed. Mickey Seven is a radical extremist and a mad bomber! And the fact that we share a lot of the same beliefs makes it scarier! She was protesting a war. Who's more anti-war than me? Does that mean it's in me to do the kind of things she has?

It's even harder for Eli. For better or worse, we now know who we are. He hasn't found a match yet, and it's becoming more and more obvious who he's going to be.

We identify Farouk al Fayed, the kidnapper, as seventh grader Freddie Cinta (*love* in Indonesian). Last on the list is C. J. Rackoff, swindler, embezzler, and Ponzi schemer. We agree on him right away, even though the youngest picture of him shows him in his twenties.

"Hector," Malik barely whispers. "Wouldn't you know he'd wind up a scuzzy little cheat, using his brains to rip people off."

Believe it or not, he says it kind of fondly.

"At least we don't have to tell him what a stinker he is," Tori offers.

"Doesn't matter," Malik murmurs sadly. "Hector was smart. He would have known what was in his own heart. Maybe that's why he was such a sad sack—just like this Rackoff guy. Look, according to this, his biggest complaint in jail is that he never gets any visitors."

"Like people should be lining up to spend time with a low-life con artist like him," I put in.

"But that's *exactly* Hector," Malik insists. "Always bent out of shape because he was being left out, or he wasn't getting his fair share of something. Poor shrimp." He lapses into a melancholy silence.

Eli's attention is still on the iPad. "There are three left," he observes in a flat tone. "Margaret and Penelope"—he takes a deep breath—"and me."

I understand what he's talking about. We don't have all the names, but the last remaining male could only be the clone of Bartholomew Glen. We've learned pretty grim things about ourselves, but Eli's lesson must be the toughest. Nothing could be more awful than finding out you're an exact copy of the Crossword Killer.

I want to say something to him, make him feel better, but the right words won't come. It's not my fault. Mickey Seven isn't the touchy-feely type.

Tori places a reassuring hand on his shoulder. "You're not your DNA," she offers gently. "None of us are."

Eli nods, but you can tell he's really devastated. "Maybe that's why my dad was so strict with me. He knew who I was and what I might turn into."

"When it comes to bad, our parents don't take a backseat to anybody," Malik assures him.

Even though nothing has changed, it suddenly comes over me: What are we doing in this sick town? "Just because there's nobody here doesn't mean they won't come back. Let's get out of here."

"The factory?" Tori asks.

"No, Serenity. This isn't our home anymore, and it never really was. Let's go."

Malik nods. "I'm with Laska. We've already learned everything we're going to. I vote we bounce. Happy Valley gives me the creeps."

"We don't have anywhere to bounce to," Eli reminds us.

"We came here for proof. We picked up a lot of information, but none of it proves anything."

We turn to Tori.

"What are you looking at me for?" she demands.

"Yvonne-Marie Delacroix would know what to do," says Malik.

"But I'm not her!"

"You've been the best at figuring out our next move," I tell her. "I don't care where we go so long as it's out of Serenity, and soon."

Tori seems stricken for an instant, and then a focused intensity takes over. "Poor C. J. Rackoff doesn't get any visitors," she muses. "I'll bet it would make his day if we stopped by and introduced ourselves."

"C. J. Rackoff?" Malik is incredulous. "Doesn't it feel bad enough to lose Hector without having to go look at his middle-aged evil twin?"

"Think," Tori prompts. "Rackoff goes back to the very beginning of Project Osiris. Maybe he knows about it. And even if he doesn't, he still might remember the day someone came and took a piece of him to make Hector."

She has all our attention now. The trail, which seemed completely cold just a few minutes ago, has several new possibilities. The DNA donors—of course!

Eli's fingers dance over the tablet. "C. J. Rackoff is serving seven consecutive twenty-year sentences at the Kefauver Federal Detention Facility in the Texas panhandle, near a town called Haddonfield." He opens a map program in a small window. "A little more than three hundred miles from here."

I may be the reckless one, thanks to Mickey Seven. But for once, I have something cautious to say. "We can't take the pool truck all that way. It must have been reported stolen by now."

"Don't worry about that," grins Malik. "I've got it covered."

20

MALIK BRUDER

By the time we roll out of Happy Valley that night, the blue Splash! truck is white. Cardboard has been taped over the hole in the glass we made breaking in. The *F* in the license plates has been changed to an *E*, and the 6 is now an 8. On the side is the logo of the New Mexico Pinto Bean Consortium, which Frieden found on the internet. Hats off to Torific—she really is great at art. If some nosy cop happens to pull alongside us on the highway, no way he'll be able to tell it's not the real thing. I wonder if Yvonne-Marie Delacroix could do that.

We leave Happy Valley pretty much the way we found it, except we take a load of clothes and some pillows and blankets in case we have to sleep in the truck. One other difference: the Laska house has its windows bashed out, courtesy of Amber, who likes to make a statement. Mickey Seven would be proud. The pool stuff is crammed into the Pritels' garage, along with a note apologizing for stealing the truck. Frieden has a thing about sorrys. Maybe he's trying to make up for being the clone of you-know-who.

I'm at the wheel, since I have the best chance of passing for old enough to drive. The minute tiny Serenity disappears from my side mirror, I know this is good-bye forever. In the back, I can hear Torific sniffling a little, but not much compared to the water works from the last time. It's not that long since we first broke out of Happy Valley, but we've changed a lot since then. It's not so much that we're tougher, although the outside world isn't as alien to us anymore. We're just not who we used to be, when our families were the most important things in our lives. Eli, Amber, and Tori will figure more in how I turn out than Mom, Dad, or anyone from Serenity ever will. I'm not an adult yet, but the kid part of my life is definitely over. For most people, this probably happens very gradually. We're not most people. In the normal sense, we're barely even people. We blasted out of childhood on a runaway cone truck.

Old County Six is so deserted that it seems like a waste of time that we bothered to paint the truck. Eventually, though, we get on Route 412 and pass the occasional car. Nobody looks twice at a home paint job on the Pinto Bean Express.

We've brought along a lot of snacks—everything we could scrounge out of four houses, mostly junk food. The idea is the fewer times we have to stop, the less chance someone will notice that we're four kids without a driver—a real licensed one, anyway. The problem is that most of that stuff is so salty that we're dying of thirst before we're even halfway to the Texas border. Then Laska gives us this long lecture about proper hydration that makes us even thirstier. We tough it out.

Although we can go without water, the truck likes a little gas every now and then. As we watch the needle edging toward E, it starts to sink in that we need a pit stop.

We pull into a service station just past a town called Clayton. I make a point of being nowhere near the wheel by the time the attendant saunters over.

He's an older man in greasy coveralls, and he looks me up and down as he pumps the gas. "Where's the driver?"

I motion vaguely toward the bathroom. "How much do we owe you?"

The pump clicks off, and he works the trigger until the readout shows an even eighty-two dollars. I hand over the cash, wondering if Tamara Dunleavy might have been a little more generous in what her driver stuck into our backpacks. Nobody thought much about the price of gas in Happy Valley, where a half-mile walk got you anywhere you wanted to go and then some.

I pay up and wait for the guy to bug off. In alarm, I realize that he's looking toward the bathroom door, waiting for "our driver" to appear, which clearly isn't going to happen. He'd better not be holding his breath. In the mirror, I catch sight of Eli, flashing me a "what's-the-holdup?" glance.

At that moment, the bathroom door opens and Tori steps out.

The attendant shoots me an arched eyebrow. "That's your driver?"

I'm starting to sweat. "No, of course not." I raise my voice to Tori. "Where's Dad?" Just to let her know we're in trouble. I hope she gets the message. Yvonne-Marie Delacroix would.

"He's around here somewhere," Tori replies glibly. "Dad . . . Dad?"

Amber jumps out of the truck and heads for the bathroom.

"How many of you kids are there?" the man demands.

"Four," I manage. "Our dad's taking us to Oklahoma to visit our grandma."

"In a pinto bean truck?"

I draw myself up with dignity. "This is the only car we have." If you don't count the quarter-million-dollar Bentley we ditched in Taos.

Amber enters the bathroom and pulls the door shut. Tori joins Eli back in the truck. A couple of minutes later, Laska returns and climbs aboard, casting the attendant a dazzling smile as she passes us.

The man looks exasperated. "Listen, son, I wasn't born yesterday. If you don't think I've got the brains to recognize a bunch of joyriders—hey!"

All at once, he's sprinting in the direction of the bathroom. Water is pouring out from under the wooden door.

A holler comes from the car. "Oh, here's Dad! Come on, Dad! Let's get going!"

I swear, I'm so confused that I'm actually looking around for "Dad." Then the driver door is kicked open and Laska's voice hisses, "Get in the car, stupid!"

I jump in and we squeal off down the road.

"What if he calls the police?" Eli asks anxiously.

"He might," Amber tells him. "When he's done

plunging that toilet, which isn't going to be for a while."

I picture the miniature Niagara cascading from the bathroom. "What did you flush down there?"

"Paper towels."

"How many?"

"All of them," she says with satisfaction. "And by the time he fishes it all out of the pipes we'll be long gone, right?"

I step on the gas a little harder. "I don't think he'll call the cops. We paid for the drinks; we paid for the gas. He can't even say for sure there was no adult with us. He called us joyriders. Not sure what that means, but I kind of like the sound of it."

We drive in anxious silence for a while, with me checking the mirror a lot. But when we cross into Texas, we breathe a little easier. We're not lawyers, but we have to believe that toilet clogging isn't the kind of offense you send officers into other states for.

We pass a sign saying that Haddonfield is 110 miles away. I feel a new dread beginning to build. C. J. Rackoff—he's sixty-two now, but everything about his picture screams Hector. His features, especially his stick-out ears; the way he holds his head. It's going to be hard to look at him—and not just because he's a big-time crook. If I cry in front of

Laska, I'll never live it down.

Why does it have to be Rackoff? We could just as easily have gone to see my guy. Well, not *just* as easily. According to the internet, Gus Alabaster is in a hospital medical unit in Joliet, Illinois. He has cancer, and his doctors don't think he's got much longer to live. I'd kind of like to meet him. Even though he's a bad guy, he's almost like the closest thing I'll ever have to a biological father. Plus it'd be a sneak preview of what I'm going to look like when I'm old. I wonder if he'd recognize himself at thirteen.

I have to forget it. It's not going to happen. The others voted for Rackoff because he's the closest. Mickey Seven's jail is in Florida, and Yvonne-Marie Delacroix is being held in New Jersey. Bartholomew Glen is the next closest, but he's all the way west, in California. And anyway, wild horses couldn't drag Eli to see him. I have to agree that the Crossword Killer doesn't sound like a very pleasant guy to hang out with.

It's after one a.m. when we reach downtown Haddonfield. We're in and out of it in about three seconds. It's one of those places you could easily miss, especially on a dark night.

We turn around to retrace our steps and end up missing the town *again*, this time going in the other direction.

"There's no way there's a whole prison here," says Amber firmly.

"There's no way there's a whole dog kennel here," I add.

"The prison's supposed to be outside of town," Eli reminds us. "The question is where. We can't just drive around in circles hoping to find a big jail. 'Outside' could mean forty miles."

There's only one light on in the entire place—seriously, they'd roll up the sidewalks if they had sidewalks. It's a 7-Eleven, which is good, because we ran out of snacks fifty miles ago. The best thing about being a fugitive is the junk food. Nobody lectures you about nutrition—unless you're unlucky enough to have Laska with you.

We might not have her with us much longer if she doesn't eat something.

"Hotter here," Tori notes as we head for the entrance. "The air feels heavier."

I shrug. "Texas." Different weather. Different scenery. Different states. It's hard to get used to after nearly fourteen years cooped up in the same handful of acres.

I open the door and usher the others inside.

The guy at the counter frowns when he takes in our age. "Isn't it a bit late for you kids to be out on your own?"

We let Tori do the talking. "Oh, we're not alone. Mom's

just too tired to get out of the truck. We've been driving all day."

He looks at us sympathetically. It's pretty obvious that he's put two and two together and concluded that we must be visiting someone at the prison. And it's probably not the warden. Let's face it, how many other reasons could there be to come to Haddonfield in the middle of the night?

Tori flushes. "We're trying to find the Kefauver prison. Our—uncle—" She's a pretty good actress, showing just the right mixture of sadness and embarrassment.

The man smiles. "You're almost there. It's about eight miles south of town."

"Is there a sign?" I ask.

"Trust me, you can't miss it, especially in the middle of the night. They keep a lot of lights on." He adds, "There's a little motel there. Nothing fancy, but it's clean. That's where the visitors usually stay."

He must feel really sorry for us because he gives us free Cheez Doodles. If he knew who we were cloned from we'd probably get half the store.

Back in the truck, I pull out of the lot and head south. The days of Frieden hogging all the driving are over. I think I've got kind of a knack for it. Maybe Gus Alabaster was a wheelman before he got too rich and important to drive his own car.

That clerk wasn't kidding about Kefauver being hard to miss. The sky starts glowing a couple of miles away. We crest a rise and there it is—a metropolis of buildings, towers, and walls, lit up like one of those sports stadiums on TV. The only thing in Serenity to compare it to is the Plastics Works, but it's more like twelve of those built together. And fences—inside, outside, all around the perimeter.

It's weird, but I actually feel bad for C. J. Rackoff having to live in such a place. I know he's a criminal, but he's also exactly like Hector, and Hector wouldn't deserve this. I know what you're thinking: something even worse happened to Hector. But still.

"What an awful place," Tori whispers.

"Take a good look at it," Amber says stoutly. "This is where our parents are going when we prove what they did. Or somewhere exactly like it."

"It's not just about revenge, Amber," Eli observes. "It's about making a life for ourselves."

"You worry about the life," Amber shoots back. "I'll handle the revenge."

"We're all cloned from people who are behind bars in

prisons just like this," Tori ventures timidly. "Is this how we're going to end up?"

"We were in a jail exactly like this," I remind them. "We had pools and tree houses and Contentment class, but could we leave?"

Eli points. "Take a left. There's the motel."

We turn into a parking lot that feels like gravel, but is really busted concrete. By the lights from the prison we can just make out the sign, which is not electrified: *Tumbleweed Inn.*

"No wonder nobody ever comes to visit C. J. Rackoff," comments Tori.

"As long as they have a shower," Amber counters.

The Tumbleweed Inn is a single strip of eighteen units, all grubby stucco and peeling paint. There are cars parked in front of units 4 and 7, but the office is dark and closed up tight.

"How are we supposed to get a room now?" I demand, annoyed.

"We can sleep in the truck," Eli suggests. "We brought pillows and blankets and everything."

"Not everything," Amber growls. "Not a shower. Or real beds."

"Or a bathroom," I add. "Those free Cheez Doodles aren't agreeing with me."

Tori makes the decision for us. "We got no rest in Serenity; we were too scared. We haven't had a decent night's sleep in days. We have to get into one of these rooms."

"You mean break in?" Eli questions.

"Right next door to a jail?" I put in nervously. Gus Alabaster wouldn't think twice about it, but I'm starting to wonder if I'm quite as brave as him.

"We can leave some money for the room after we—uh—check out," Tori suggests. "Come on, we *need* this."

"*And* for the damage we have to do to get in," Eli adds.

Tori shrugs. "Maybe there won't be any."

I take the truck around the back and park it where it's semihidden in a grove of trees. There are no lights in the rear, but the prison is so bright that we can see enough not to wipe out.

"There was a TV show where somebody got into a hotel just by slipping a card through the door," Amber ventures.

"We don't need that," Tori says. "Look."

We squint into the gloom. Along the row of hotel units is a line of high windows, each one propped open with a short stick.

Tori approaches the end room and turns to me. "Give me a boost."

She steps into the basket I make with my hands. I heave her up to the window. It takes some doing, because she has to remove the screen. But within two minutes, she's in. We hear her drop to the floor.

We run around the front. She's already standing there with the door open, grinning widely. "Welcome to our humble abode."

"Get that screen back in!" I snap. "They've got mosquitoes the size of B-52s around here!"

The place is a dump by Serenity standards, but with the advantage of not being in Serenity. There are two double beds—one for the girls and one for Eli and me. We give them first dibs on the shower.

By the time they come out, we're dead to the world.

21

TORI PRITEL

I wake up scared.

These days, I always wake up scared. But today's different. I'm in that dump truck in Denver and it's tipping me down into the wood chipper. The grinding noise is loud and very near, and I'm sliding, falling . . .

Heart hammering, I leap out of bed, biting my fist to keep from screaming as I struggle to get my bearings. There's no wood chipper, just an air conditioner—in great need of maintenance—a couple of doors down. I'm still in the room at the Tumbleweed Inn. The air is hot and heavy as pea soup. We don't dare use our own air conditioner, since no one is supposed to be here. Dim light filters in through the uneven venetian blinds. Not morning, not yet.

More like predawn. I check the nightstand clock. 5:16 a.m.

Amber's still asleep, sweat beaded on her brow. In the other bed, so is Malik—at least I assume that lump in the blankets is him. (I recognize the snoring.) Where's Eli?

A second later I spot him in the center of the room, still as a statue, staring at the front door.

"What?" I ask in a low voice.

"Someone's out there," he whispers hoarsely.

"Are you sure?"

"I swear I saw the doorknob turn."

I go to the window, open the blinds an inch or so, and peer outside. The walkway is deserted. I move to the other side and check the opposite direction. Nobody's there. But at the far end of the strip, I can see a splash of light spilling out of the office.

"The coast is clear," I report. "But the check-in desk is open."

He looks worried. "Do you think the clerk will be able to tell someone's in the room?"

"I don't know," I reply, "but we'd better do a little scouting around. If anybody's about to call the police on us, we need to be gone."

We kick into shoes, grab some money, and slip out the

front door. We snake around the back of the Tumbleweed Inn, confirming first that the truck is well hidden. Malik did a good job parking it in some thick trees, where it wouldn't be easily spotted by employees or guests of the motel.

The office has a high rear window, just like the rooms do. We're not worried about being heard, since an ancient air conditioner roars in there too. Eli boosts me up and I peer inside.

The clerk reminds me of my own mother (the person who posed as my mother, obviously). The resemblance puts me at ease and on edge at the same time. She's all alone at the desk, watching a tiny portable TV. I spy on her for a few seconds and conclude that there's no way she knows trespassers broke into one of her rooms last night. She looks bored—half-comatose, actually. Her attention never wavers from the small screen.

I jump down and signal Eli to start back.

"What, no room service?" he whispers.

I smother a laugh. I like being with Eli. In Serenity, we were getting to be pretty close. Malik used to tease us about being boyfriend/girlfriend, although it was nothing like that. Now we spend more time together than ever, but it's not the same, since we're always running for our lives. All at once, I realize how much I miss hanging out with him.

We're about halfway to the end of the strip building when Eli suddenly wheels. "Did you hear that?"

I turn and scan our surroundings. There's nobody around. From the front of the motel, the ice machine clunks. "Is that what you heard?"

He looks doubtful. "Maybe. It's probably just me. I'm pretty stressed these days. For all I know, the doorknob never moved either."

"We're all on edge," I assure him.

But as we reach the pavement of the side parking lot, *I* hear it—and it's definitely not the ice machine. Scuffling footsteps, dislodging rocks and chunks of fractured concrete. Yet when we turn around, no one's there.

Is someone *stalking* us?

We're not walking anymore. We run the rest of the way to our room and duck inside.

"Wake up!" Eli cries at the sleepers.

They're out of bed like a shot. "What is it?" Malik babbles, blinking wildly.

"We're not sure," I confess.

His brow lowers. "You woke me up for not sure?

Come back when you're sure!"

Only half-awake, Amber stumbles toward the bathroom. Her eyes aren't open yet, so she doesn't see it. There's a face at the window, pale and indistinct through the dusty screen.

I scream. That wakes Amber up, and the guys come running. But by that time the face is gone.

"We've got to disappear!" I hiss. "They're after us! He was looking in the window!"

"Who?" Eli demands.

"I couldn't tell. He has to be really tall, though, if he could see in! Maybe one of the Purples."

"I'm not sticking around to find out!" Malik declares.

We jam our stuff into our backpacks. I peer through the venetians. "Coast is clear."

"On three," whispers Malik. "One . . . two . . ."

He hurls the door open and leaps outside. But instead of making his escape, he trips over something and crashes sprawling to the pavement. We hear a muffled *"Oof,"* definitely not from Malik.

Eli picks up the nearest weapon, a porcelain table lamp, yanking the plug from the wall. Brandishing it like a club, he springs after Malik to fight for our freedom. He lifts it high, ready to deliver a devastating blow.

Malik's eyes bulge. *"Stop!"* He grabs the lamp in mid-stroke.

Amber and I scramble into the fray. We gawk. We goggle.

Lying on the ground, stunned, is Hector Amani.

22

MALIK BRUDER

My head explodes. Seriously, that's what it feels like.

Hector—I never thought I'd see the little shrimp again! I shouldn't be seeing him now! He *died*!

The others are just as blown away. Eli drops the lamp, which shatters on the concrete.

Half to prove to myself that he isn't a ghost, I throw my arms around Hector and squeeze.

"Not so hard," he gasps. "I can't breathe!"

"You're not supposed to breathe!" My voice comes out unsteady. "You're supposed to be dead!" There's wetness running down my cheeks. I think I might be crying. Impossible—Gus Alabaster never cries! But I don't care. I can't process any information beyond the impossible fact that Hector's okay.

"We don't have time for this," Tori hisses. "There's a Purple around. We saw him looking into our room."

"That was *me*," Hector rasps.

Tori shakes her head. "That guy had to be six-foot-five."

"I was standing on boxes," Hector explains. "I had to make sure it was really you."

"Why didn't you say something?" Amber demands

He's sheepish. "I got so excited to see you that I fell. I came around to knock on the door, and Malik plowed me over." He rubs his brow. "Elbowed me in the face."

We get him ice for his forehead, but not before the hugging happens—first the girls, and then Frieden. I go again for good measure, and this time I really crush him. He's feeling it, but he doesn't complain. We both understand that coming back from the dead is a pretty big deal.

It's time for some major catching up. Hector lies on one of the beds, holding the towel-wrapped cubes to his bruise, and rakes us with a resentful glare. "Thanks a lot, you guys, for saving yourselves and leaving me alone to die in the woods."

Only the shrimp could make me so happy and so exasperated all at once. "Some things never change. Complain, complain, complain. We *looked* for you, man. We screamed the forest down until the cars started up from Happy Valley."

"It's true," Eli confirms. "When we couldn't find you, we thought you went over the side with the truck. You were still hanging on when I jumped."

"We had to drag Malik away," Tori adds. "He was out of his mind. I've never seen him like that before."

"And you see the thanks I get." I glare at Hector, my cheeks hot. "I'm the one who should be ticked off at you, letting us think you're dead. I wasted a lot of sad on your unworthy butt!"

"It's like Eli said," Hector admits. "I hung on too long, and by the time I jumped, the truck had already broken through the barrier. I rolled into a tree and I must have got knocked out. It was good luck—if the tree hadn't been there, I would have gone all the way to the bottom and burned up in the explosion."

"How come the Purples didn't catch you?" asks Amber.

"I ran into the woods and climbed a tree. They searched like crazy, but they never looked up. I could have spit down on them a couple of times. I heard them talking. They were pretty sure we all died in the wreck. I guess traffic cones burn really slow, because the flames went on for days, and they couldn't get close enough to figure out we weren't there."

"Yeah, okay," says Malik. "But how did you get *here*?"

"Don't rush me. I'm telling the story. So I stay in the woods as long as I can, thinking maybe you guys will come back for me." He shakes his head. "Maybe some people can survive in the wild, but not me. You swallow ten million berries and all you get is a stomachache. Once I chased this rabbit for hours, but when I finally caught him, I couldn't figure out how to make him die. So I let him go. I'd barely eaten in days. And I thought, whatever they do to me in Serenity, it can't be as bad as starving to death. So I walked back into town. But you're never going to believe this: Nobody was there."

Eli nods. "We escaped with their secret, and they ran away."

"What could I do?" Hector continues. "I went home. At least there was food. I ate everything. I was spooning cold peas out of the can. I poked around, looking for clues about where everybody went, and I found my mom's private diary. This name kept coming up—C. J. Rackoff. She compared me to this guy in at least a dozen places. I remembered there's real internet near the factory, so I took our laptop over there. He's a big-time crook—famous, even. And you know what? I think he's the guy I'm cloned from."

Eli, the girls, and I exchange meaningful glances. Say

what you want about Hector—and I do—nobody can deny that he's smart. Our paths were totally different and still the facts led the five of us to the exact same place. Surely that means we're on the right track.

"Anyway," Hector concludes. "The website said C. J. Rackoff was in jail here, so I gathered up all the loose money I could find and walked out of town."

"Three hundred miles?" Tori challenges.

"Of course not. I hitchhiked. At first, people thought I was running away, so I had this idea. I started saying I was *already* away, and was trying to get home. Who wouldn't help a kid get home? Whatever the next town on the sign was, that's where I pretended to live. It takes a long time, but eventually you get where you're going."

"How did you find *us*?" Eli probes.

Hector shrugs. "You can't just knock on the front gate of a prison. This hotel is the only place around here. I swear, when I saw you guys, I thought it was a hallucination."

Crazy story? Sure. But it's a lot easier to swallow than the series of events that brought us four to the Tumbleweed Inn.

His eyes grow wider and wider as we fill him in on what we've been through since the breakout. It spills out of us in bits and pieces like we barely believe it ourselves. We do barely believe it ourselves.

When we get to the part in Jackson Hole, and how we cut out our neck implants, he looks squeamish and feels for his own. There's no bump like Amber's, but upon closer inspection of his skin, we find the telltale scar, long healed, in exactly the right spot.

Hector is confused. "If I still have the chip, why didn't the barrier get me?"

Eli shrugs. "They would have had to turn it off when they took the other clones out of Serenity. Or maybe they never fixed it after we wrecked it when we broke out."

That annoys me. "Are you saying I went through that torture for nothing?"

Amber rolls her eyes. "We all went through 'that torture,' not just you."

"Which doesn't change the fact that *I* went through torture! I was bleeding, you know!"

Hector grins. "I see leaving Serenity hasn't changed what a big baby you are."

I glare at him. "Real funny coming from a kid who can't even get killed and make it stick."

"Hector, we're so glad that you're okay," Tori tells him. "It was agony to go on without you, and we thought about you every minute—especially Malik."

You know what? I'm actually grateful to her for that.

Somebody had to say it. I never would have.

It strikes a note with Hector, who flushes. "I thought about you guys a lot too," he mumbles uncomfortably.

"Right," I dig at him. "You thought about how we abandoned you, how everything bad that happened was our fault. We were basically starring in another exciting episode of your favorite show, *Oh, Poor Me.*"

"Yeah, but it worked out okay, right? We're all together again."

"The freak show's back in business," I agree.

Here we are, five escaped clones huddled in a cheap motel room outside Haddonfield, Texas. Less than a quarter mile away, behind high walls, barbed wire, and iron bars is a connection to the sinister experiment that's responsible for our existence.

The truth is very close. We can almost taste it.

23

HECTOR AMANI

I remember it like it just happened five minutes ago. Serenity Day. The escape. The speeding cone transport. And then darkness.

I woke up to a splitting headache. Not the sickness and pain of the invisible barrier. My head was just killing me. I put my hand up to my temple, and it came away bloody. What did I expect after jumping off a runaway truck?

I struggled to my feet—and very nearly keeled over and rolled down a steep embankment. At the last second, I flailed my arms and grabbed onto a tree trunk—probably the same one that did a number on my skull. In a wild moment of vertigo, I pieced together what must have happened. I got off the truck at the last second, tumbled over the side, and whacked my head on this tree. It hurt like crazy, but it was a blessing. It was the only thing that kept me from rolling all the way to the bottom. With my luck, the truck would have landed right on top of me. It was down in the valley, shooting flames thirty feet in the air—thus explaining why the barrier was gone.

Where were the others? Dead in the fire? For a moment I panicked. Then it came back to me. They all got off the truck. I was the last one.

"Malik!" I called. "Eli! Tori! Amber!"

I got no answer.

It was too steep to walk, so I got down on all fours and crawled back up to the road. *"Malik!"*

They couldn't all be dead! If I made it, they made it. I shouted at the top of my lungs, which sent me into coughing fits. I must have swallowed a lot of dirt before the tree coldcocked me.

"Come on, you guys! Don't do this to me!"

My pleas echoed in the night.

I recall my exact logic that night: *If they survived the crash, there can be only one possible explanation for what's happening. They've abandoned me.*

It was the loneliest, emptiest, most awful feeling I've ever known.

And then: *Why are you so shocked? You've always sort of*

known that the only person who cares about you is you. Even among the Serenity "parents," yours were the only ones who couldn't manage to work up any affection for the baby clone they were given to raise!

I was absolutely convinced that my one miscalculation was allowing myself to believe that the others were my real friends.

Yet here they are with me now, sitting on hard chairs in the visiting room inside Kefauver prison. They say they were sad when they thought I was dead. According to Tori, Malik even cried. I want to believe that so much.

I'm grateful to them for this, though: I would never have the guts to face C. J. Rackoff alone. They're the only people in the world with a hope of understanding. They have their own C. J. Rackoffs out there somewhere—criminals just as sleazy, and scary, and horrible. Maybe more. They told me about Bartholomew Glen. Poor Eli.

A key jiggles in a lock at the back of the room. That's one thing there's no shortage of in jail—locks. It's easy to get on the visitors list at Kefauver. You just tell them how to spell your name. But that's the last easy thing about it. We must have passed through ten layers of security to get this far. That plus a metal detector and a personal search that was not pleasant. I'm ticklish. And this is only medium security, where they put the swindlers and embezzlers. What have they got at maximum? A moat with hungry piranhas?

The door swings open, hinges squeaking. Tori grabs my shoulder and gives me a comforting squeeze.

I see the guard first, and then *he* walks in. He's old and bald and not very tall, with glasses and a fringe of salt-and-pepper hair around stick-out ears. My first thought is: *There must be some mistake.* This guy looks nothing like me. There's no way I'm cloned from him. We couldn't even be distant cousins, much less identical people.

He pans the room, his eyes magnified behind Coke-bottle glasses. His expression remains bland until the supersize eyes land on me. All at once, he breaks into a big grin and laughs out loud.

"Would you look at that? They did it. Those crazy fools went ahead and did it!"

"What do you mean?" I quaver, even though I know exactly what he means. He recognizes me, all right. He's *been* me.

So this is it—the source of what I'm made of, my "parent" more fully than any biological mother or father. It could be a warm, completing moment, but I just feel like a freak, and even more alone than before.

Rackoff turns to the guard. "Haven't you got a date?"

The guard seems uncertain.

"These kids are my spiritual advisors. You're interfering with my freedom of religion."

"I'll be right outside," the man tells us with a meaningful look. "All you have to do is holler."

"What do you mean, Mr. Rackoff?" Eli asks as soon as the door shuts behind the guard.

"Let me tell you kids a story. Years ago, the powers that be tell me I've got a visitor. Felix Somebody. I don't know any Felix, but I've got no plans that day, or any day, as you can see." He indicates the prison setting around us. "Very interesting man. He's got some billionaire backing him, and he says he can cut off a little piece of skin and make a whole new me for an experiment he's got going on. He offers me money. Like there's anything to spend it on in here. Besides, I've got enough stashed away in secret bank accounts to buy and sell his billionaire. So he tries another approach, tells me I'll be passing on my genes to future generations. So I point out, in case he hasn't noticed, that I'm a sawed-off little wing nut, and people hate me on sight." He turns to me. "Sorry, kid."

"I'm used to it," I tell him in resignation.

Malik opens his mouth to protest, but shuts it again.

Amber speaks up. "What made you decide to go along with Project Osiris?"

Rackoff brightens. "That's right. He said something about Osiris. Anyway, I did it for the brownies."

We all stare at him.

"You can't put a million bucks in the soda machine. But brownies—from a real New York bakery—*that's* something to look forward to in a place where there's nothing to look forward to. Twice a week, someone ships me a care package from Sarabeth's in Chelsea Market. Pure heaven. They make these double chocolate brownies to die for."

Malik goes into a coughing spasm, and I know he's thinking of his mom's chocolate brownies, which I used to love. As mean as he could sometimes be, he always invited me over when Mrs. Bruder was baking.

"They're my favorite too," I volunteer timidly.

"No kidding." It's not exactly a chip-off-the-old-block moment, but he seems pleased we have this tiny random thing in common. "So, as I was saying, those shipments came like clockwork, until about a week ago. Felix reneged on our deal."

Eli clears his throat. "I don't think you're going to get any more brownies from Project Osiris. What they did was very illegal. When we escaped, they had to go into hiding."

The eyes—*my* eyes—narrow. Do I really look like that?

He says, "I always figured I couldn't be the only one. So you're all—like him?" Meaning me.

"The word is *clones*," Amber tells him. "No point trying to sugarcoat it."

Rackoff takes it all in. "So after this Felix was done with me, he had some other stops to make. All convicts like me?"

"They wanted criminal masterminds," Eli supplies.

"Masterminds," he repeats. "Never thought of myself as a mastermind. I'm just someone with a knack for reading the wind, and positioning myself so money blows in my direction."

I've been pretty quiet in the presence of the person I was cloned from, but something about his casual attitude bugs me. "It's not funny, you know. How'd you like to discover your whole life is a lie, the people you thought were your parents are mad scientists, and you only exist to be part of some experiment?"

He looks at me with a little more respect. "I guess that would be a downer. Then again, I'm in a cage, so I'm living proof that bad things happen to people. Is there a purpose to this visit, or is it just supposed to be a family reunion?"

He's a jerk, I think to myself. Which might actually mean that I'm a jerk. That wouldn't surprise me.

"Mr. Rackoff," Eli begins, "cloning criminals is more than just a crime. It's cruel. There are eleven of us; we have no parents, and maybe we're not a hundred percent human. We don't want to be part of their experiment anymore, but there's nothing else for us. We need your help."

"*My* help?" he echoes, looking interested.

"No one's ever going to believe our story without proof," Eli goes on. "We tried once, and ended up having to escape from the police. And without protection from the authorities, it's only a matter of time before Project Osiris tracks us down. But you can prove our case. You and Hector have the same DNA—that can be confirmed in a lab. Add to that what you know about Felix and the beginning of Osiris, and they'd have to listen to us then."

Rackoff takes all this in. "They would at that," he says, impressed.

"So you'll help us?" Tori prompts.

"No."

"Why not?" I wail, so loudly that I see the guard peeking in to make sure we're okay.

"I'm just asking myself: How does this make my life better? Does it shorten my sentence? Does it move me to a better cell? Does it keep me off the work detail here, making mailbags, stitching canvas till my fingers bleed? It doesn't even bring back my brownies. I'll bet none of you kids has so much as a credit card."

"What about justice?" Amber demands.

He shrugs. "That's what makes *your* life better. Me, I'm not too thrilled with justice."

I have one last trump card, and I play it. "Can't you do it for me? I know you're not my dad, but you're the nearest thing I've got. In a way, it's even closer, because we're identical."

"Right," Rackoff approves. "We *are* identical. So you should already know what I'd need to cooperate with you on this deal."

"Come off it!" Malik protests on my behalf. "Hector can't read minds."

C. J. Rackoff is right, though. I'm not sure if it's mind reading, or having the same genes, but I know what he wants. He wants out of this place.

"It's not possible," I barely whisper.

He shrugs. "Suit yourselves. If you can break me out of jail, you can have my DNA, and my testimony, and my undying gratitude. If you can't, we've got nothing left to talk about."

"You're crazy!" Malik exclaims. "How are we going to get you out of here? We're just kids!"

"You're not just kids," he amends in a pleasant tone. "You're masterminds. I know what I'm capable of. The rest of you must be spliced off some heavy hitters too. You need my help? First I need yours."

It's shocking but, on second thought, it's pretty much exactly what I would have said.

24

TORI PRITEL

They all look at me when it's time to come up with a plan. I have no idea why. I'm an artist. I'm observant, and I have a good memory for detail. That's it. I don't know anything about prison breaks (and I'm proud of that).

"First of all, why are we even considering doing this?" I ask them. "If anybody ever belonged behind bars, it's C. J. Rackoff. We already know he's a criminal. But even worse, he's a terrible person!"

"He's the only one who can help us," Eli reasons.

"Not true," I point out. "What about Yvonne-Marie Delacroix? Or Mickey Seven? Or Gus Alabaster?" I stop short at mentioning Bartholomew Glen, because I can't imagine him helping us to anything other than an early death.

"All those guys are hundreds of miles away—maybe

thousands," Eli points out. "We could cross the whole country only to be told they refuse to see us, or they're not allowed visitors. And they're all in maximum security as dangerous offenders. It's Rackoff or nobody."

"I know he's a bad guy," Hector tells me. "But if he's me—well, I can't explain it, but there's nothing inside me that anyone would have to be afraid of."

"He's a saint," agrees Malik. "Unless you've got twenty-five cents in your pocket, and then he won't rest until he's got it."

As usual, Amber is the one who boils our choice down to the simplest possible terms. "Rackoff deserves to stay in jail. But if we've got any chance at a future, we have to get him out. It's that simple."

"*Can* we get him out?" asks Hector nervously. "That's a real prison, with high walls and armed guards. It's impossible."

But when I run my mind over the information Rackoff gave us about Kefauver, I don't see impossibilities; I see challenges. And the tougher the challenges, the more I want to find a way to beat them. I know it comes from Yvonne-Marie Delacroix, but I don't care. It's more than simple determination; it's almost an itch I have to scratch.

"*Almost* impossible," I amend. "Everything seems too

hard when you look at the whole operation. The trick is to break it down into individual parts. The big picture can't be impossible if none of the little parts are. You just have to do everything exactly right, in exactly the right order."

In other words, *almost impossible* is a synonym for *ever-so-slightly possible.*

That's how I end up in charge of a prison break.

Our tiny motel room feels even smaller now that there are five of us. Gathered around the small desk, Amber makes notes on what we know about Kefauver:

1.) Prison workshop produces mailbags for US Postal Service.
2.) Prison laundry is directly next to workshop.
3.) Prison hospital is directly above laundry.
4.) Prisoners can get special permission for supervised picnics with visitors.

The workshop is obviously the key. The mailbags they make for the post office are the only things that leave Kefauver without passing through all those security checkpoints.

"Maybe we could smuggle him out with one of the shipments when he's on work detail," Malik suggests.

Eli shakes his head. "No good. Rackoff was really specific on that. They're nuts about counting heads every time a truck leaves the loading dock."

That gives me an idea "We'll have to get him into a shipment when he's *not* on work detail."

Hector's brow furrows, making him look more like Rackoff than ever. "But you're not allowed to wander around anywhere you please. The guards know where you're supposed to be every minute of every day. That's what Rackoff hates the most. You can't burp without somebody knowing what you had for lunch."

"That's what we'll use against them," I say triumphantly.

"Haven't you got that backward?" Eli asks. "Isn't that what they use against the inmates to make sure they're always accounted for?"

"The more confident the guards are that they've got Rackoff covered, the more we can move him around. They won't be looking for him because they'll always be sure he's somewhere else."

The plan begins to come together. In some ways, it reminds me of our escape from Serenity—with some important differences. Back then, we had the element of surprise on our side. But a real prison is always prepared for the possibility that one of the "guests" might try to make an early exit.

The main difference is this: When we left Serenity, we had weeks to prepare, time enough to ensure every detail had been accounted for. Here in Texas, the clock is running out on us as surely as we can hear its *tick-tock* speeding up. At the Tumbleweed Inn, we've stopped using the front door, sneaking in and out via the bathroom window. Even so, it's only a matter of time before someone notices that room 18 isn't as empty as it's supposed to be. And our truck is a time bomb just waiting to be spotted. We have to do this tomorrow, which means there's no way we'll be able to plan for everything.

We'll be flying by the seat of our pants.

Two things we'll need to make this work: split-second timing, and a picnic lunch. We can't get either of those at the motel. (All they sell in the vending machine here are mini-packets of Tylenol, stale shrink-wrapped muffins, and dental floss.) That presents the problem of taking out the truck without attracting attention.

The prison has an ear-splitting siren that can be heard

for miles around. It's probably the escape alarm, but yesterday at exactly noon, they ran it for about ten seconds. Close by (at the Tumbleweed Inn, for instance) it gets so loud that you feel your internal organs vibrating. We're guessing it's a daily test.

We're in the truck at 11:59. At the first onslaught of sound, Malik stomps on the gas, and we wheel out from behind the trees, our engine's roar completely covered by the blaring siren. We bump up onto the pavement and speed across the parking lot. By the time the test is over, we're already pulling onto the road.

"Every bank robber needs a good getaway driver," Malik tosses over his shoulder at me.

"If I meet any bank robbers, I'll tell them that," I remind him irritably. (I'm not a bank robber; I just happen to be cloned from one.)

Our destination is the variety store in Haddonfield. I'm the only one with a watch, which means we need four more. And there's a supermarket next door where we can get sandwich stuff and drinks for the picnic.

Amber goes crazy at the salad bar. It's the first veggies she's had access to in a long time. (I guess this means her goal weight is on again.)

We're on our way back to the motel, Malik at the wheel,

when we pass a small roadside diner just on the edge of town.

"Stop!" I scream right in Malik's ear.

Shocked, he jams on the brakes, and we fishtail onto the soft shoulder. "What?"

"That diner over there—the Bearclaw!"

He's mad. "Thanks a lot, Miss Keep-a-Low-Profile! I left half our tire treads on the road, and squealed the town down! Way to go!"

"Look—in the parking lot!"

There sits a large windowless cargo van, white, with the logo of the United States Postal Service stamped on the side.

"Big deal," says Malik. "A mail truck."

"I don't think that's a mail truck," I tell him excitedly. "We saw mail trucks in Denver. They're smaller, with an open door so the carrier can jump in and out and make deliveries. I think this is the one Rackoff told us about—the one that goes to Kefauver every weekday to pick up the mail bags from the workshop."

They listen to me—or maybe it's Yvonne-Marie Delacroix they're listening to. Either way, they're willing to follow my lead. This could be the last piece of the puzzle.

We park a quarter mile away so we can enter the diner

on foot, waving and calling, "Bye, Mom" to an imaginary lift. It's a nice clean-looking diner, deserted except for one waitress and one customer, a young guy in a postal uniform. He's at the counter, having coffee and complaining about the cruller, which is "not up to your usual standards."

"I know, George," the waitress apologizes. "We're baking tonight, so everything should be nice and fresh for you tomorrow."

"Make some bear claws," the USPS guy requests. "That's what you're famous for."

We settle ourselves at a booth, and order Cokes all around, except for Amber, who gets sparkling water. At the side of our table, built into the wall, there's a small console with a coin slot and a booklet of plastic-covered lists of what look like titles and names.

"What's that?" whispers Malik.

Eli turns the metal crank, scrolling through the different pages. "Snoop Dogg?" he reads, brow furrowing. "Imagine Dragons? Hootie and the Blowfish?"

I shrug. We've gotten pretty good at decoding the outside world, but every now and then something comes along that we really don't have a clue about.

"Ask the waitress," Amber suggests.

I shake my head. "If this is a common thing everybody

knows, it would draw attention. I just hope it isn't important, like you're supposed to use it to pay your bill."

Luckily, the USPS guy (George) bails us out by putting a quarter in a similar console at the counter. He presses a few buttons and a song begins to play in the Bearclaw.

Light dawns. "It's a jukebox," I tell the others in a low voice. "I've read about them in books. You pay money to hear the music you want."

"Really? These are songs?" Amber peers through the plastic cover. "'Da Bomb.' Who'd write a song about a bomb?"

"Maybe *you* would," Malik offers sweetly. "Isn't Mickey Seven the mad bomber?"

"Big talk from the gangster DNA—"

"Shhh!" I cut her off and make eye contact with the postal worker. "I love this song. It must be nice to finish your route early and have a little time to relax."

"Oh, I'm not a carrier," he replies. "I'm picking up new product from the shop at Kefauver."

I'm confused. "New product?"

"Mailbags," he explains. "The prisoners churn them out by the hundreds. Don't know why we need so many of them, but every day they've got a new load for me."

The waitress laughs. "You can set your watch by

George. Every day, one thirty, coffee and a bear claw, Taylor Swift on the jukebox. One fifty—out the door. And twenty minutes later, tooting the horn and waving at me as he moves on."

"They're nuts about their timetable at the prison," George explains. "If I'm sixty seconds early, they make me wait."

"And if you're sixty seconds late?" the waitress asks with a smile.

He rolls his eyes. "The warden's a stickler. I don't like to cross that guy. I just make my pickup and get on my way, all nice and boring."

I look meaningfully around the table at my four accomplices. I'm still not sure exactly how things are going to go tomorrow, but this much is certain: it won't be boring.

None of us get much sleep that night; I'm pretty sure I get the least of all. Just the enormity of what we're about to do has us totally cowed. We may have the right stuff to be criminal masterminds, but we're not there yet. (I hope we never are.) Maybe Yvonne-Marie Delacroix stayed up the night before a big robbery with prejob jitters. Anyway, she wasn't twelve.

Eventually, the others doze off, and I stay up, tossing

and turning beside Amber. When they made me the chief planner, they made me the chief stresser too. Is that even a real word? If not, it should be. I'm stressing like crazy over this.

I watch them for a few minutes—Amber next to me, Eli and Malik in the other bed, Hector wrapped up in a blanket on the floor despite the heat. In the distance, air conditioners roar on.

I'm proud of the way they rely on me, but nervous too. I don't want to let them down, because in our case, a letdown means total disaster. Any kind of arrest would be the end of the road for us. Even if, by some miracle, the prison authorities decided to let us go, they wouldn't cut five unsupervised kids completely loose in the world. And when they looked around for our families, there would be the Purple People Eaters, waiting to take us "home."

Another reason it's so hard to sleep: because I put together most of the plan, I understand better than anybody what could go wrong. There are a million variables, and that's just with *us*. What about C. J. Rackoff? Any swindler successful enough to count as a mastermind can't be considered trustworthy. Besides, he doesn't know about any of this. And he won't until it's already in motion.

I must doze off out of sheer exhaustion, because the

next thing I know, I awake with a start, and the door is opening! I see a sliver of the night outside—*and the menacing silhouette of an intruder entering Room 18!*

I consider waking the others. If this is the Purples moving in on us, we're all going to have to fight for our freedom. But that would just inform the enemy that I'm awake, and I see him. I need to strike now, while I've got the element of surprise.

I reach down and pick up the first thing my hand closes on—a metal wastebasket. In one motion, I'm out of bed, across the room, and swinging my weapon at the shadowy figure.

Whack!

"Ow!"

Wait a minute —

(I know that *ow*.)

"Eli?" I glance over at the other bed, and see the outline of only one person under the blanket.

"Jeez, Tori, you nearly took my head off!" he hisses.

I'm frantic now. "Are you all right?"

"What's this sticky stuff? Is it blood?"

I hustle him into the bathroom, and turn on the light. It *is* blood, but just a trickle from a small impact cut above his left eye. It's easy enough to clean up, but he'll probably have a bruise tomorrow. "What were you doing out of the room?" I ask.

"I couldn't sleep," he admits. "I kept thinking that, when it's time for me to hack into the computer system at Kefauver, what if I can't make it work from my iPad? So I went to the computer room next to the office."

"And?" I prompt.

"Well," he explains, "the main site has a lot of security, but the hospital's different because they have to exchange medical records and information with outside doctors and clinics. I can get in—that's if I don't have amnesia from being bashed in the head."

"Sorry about that." I flush. "If things go bad tomorrow—if it turns out, you know, this is the last time we see each other—" Suddenly, I can't finish my own thought. I'm not sure I ever knew what I was trying to tell him. Maybe this: *We went through something pretty terrible. We're still going through it. The one thing that's made it bearable is that you've been there.*

(I could never say that out loud.)

He takes my hand and squeezes it, holding on so long that I actually count: *One . . . two . . . three . . .*

"It'll be fine," he tells me finally.

I wonder if he believes it any more than I do.

* * *

Lugging the food bag between us, Hector and I cross the highway and start up the drive for the front gate of Kefauver Federal Detention Facility. The time is 12:15. We've all synchronized watches.

"Nice day for a picnic, huh?" Hector says nervously.

I look around as if noticing the weather for the first time. It *is* a nice day—cloudless sky, sunny, with that inevitable Texas heat. It occurs to me for the first time—what would we do with our picnic if it was pouring rain? Is that how good this plan is? How many other important things didn't I think of?

Kefauver policy may allow picnics, but that doesn't stop the gate sentry from searching our food bag with everything short of an electron microscope. After he paws through it all, he invites us to move on. As we proceed through the security procedures, our bag is unpacked and searched twice more, X-rayed once, and passed through two metal detectors. It definitely spoils the picnic mood. But, of course, this has never been about lunch for Hector and me. We're scared out of our minds.

Finally, we're standing in the same visitors' meeting room we were in yesterday as C. J. Rackoff is escorted to our side.

"The crowd's getting smaller," he comments. "Was it something I said?"

I try to laugh, but it comes out a strangled sound. "We brought you a picnic lunch, Uncle C.J."

He looks to the guard, who nods. "You're approved for the outdoor tables. Let's go."

We're marched down echoing corridors, and through steel security doors. I catch a few questioning glances from Rackoff, but luckily he knows enough to keep his mouth shut. Hector has always been the smartest of us, and this must be where he gets it.

There's only one way to describe the picnic area: secure. There's a little grass—half a knoll between thirty-foot fences topped with razor wire. One of the guard towers looks directly down on the wooden tables. It's not indoors and behind bars, but it might as well be.

At least they leave us alone. As we unload the sandwiches and drinks, I drop a napkin and stoop to pick it up. What I'm really doing is checking the underside of the table for listening devices. What we have to say doesn't need to be shared with the prison authorities.

Rackoff says, "I ask for my freedom, and you bring me a sandwich. Excuse me for being a little disappointed."

"Maybe you can have both," Hector retorts.

He looks intrigued. "Tell me more."

"We'll get you out," I say in a low voice, "but only if you promise to help us tell our story to the world."

"You have my word," he replies readily.

I look to Hector, who has the best chance of anyone alive of knowing what's inside the head of this master criminal. He nods.

"Okay," I begin. "Listen carefully, because we have to get this exactly right . . ."

25

ELI FRIEDEN

I wonder how the picnic is going.

I check my watch. 1:17 p.m. By now it's in full swing, and Rackoff knows exactly what our plan is. I hope he can pull it off. He's an accomplished con man and professional liar. But let's face it—if he was that good, he wouldn't be in prison in the first place.

The parking lot of the Bearclaw is just a dirt clearing beside the tiny diner. It's back from the road and surrounded by high bushes, where we're crouched, hiding.

If that waitress is to be believed, George is due here in his post office truck in exactly thirteen minutes. I can already feel lines of sweat streaming down under my shirt. By the time George arrives, I'll be a puddle.

Malik slaps at a mosquito on his cheek. "How come

there always has to be bugs?"

"You think Gus Alabaster's afraid of mosquitoes?" Amber says in amusement.

"I'm not afraid of them. I just hate them." He takes the three-foot crowbar he's brandishing and uses it to disperse a cloud of gnats. The thing comes dangerously close to my head, and I duck. I've already been coldcocked by Tori. My face doesn't need any more rearranging.

My eyes are never far from my watch, until 1:30. "He's late—" I begin. But before the echo of my words has time to die, the USPS van is turning into the drive. The waitress is right. You *can* set your watch by George.

He pulls into the parking lot and gets out of the car, heading for the entrance to the diner.

"This is it!" whispers Malik, preparing to step out of the bushes and intercept the post office man.

An instant later, a second vehicle pulls into the Bearclaw parking lot—a Texas state trooper. I haul Malik back down into the cover of the foliage.

Malik wrestles himself free and peers through the leafy branches. George is almost at the front door. "He's getting away!"

"What are you going to do?" I demand. "Threaten him in front of a cop?"

"We'll just have to wait till he comes out," Amber decides.

"What if the cop's still here?" Malik asks frantically.

"You can't see the parking lot from the restaurant," I soothe. "We'll have to chance it. It's our only way of staying on schedule."

We cool our heels, which is almost impossible in this climate.

A few minutes later, the cop emerges carrying a candy bar and a diet Dr Pepper. He drives off. Still no sign of George, who is probably enjoying the fresh-baked bear claw he was promised yesterday.

Now we're all looking at our watches. He has to be at Kefauver in twelve minutes, so he should be coming out any second. 1:49, 1:50, 1:51 . . .

Malik starts to panic. "What happened to the guy you can set your watch by?"

"Cool your jets!" Amber exclaims, but I can see she's just as wired as he is.

And then there he is, a minute behind schedule, and walking fast to make up the time—George.

As he steps through the gap in the trees into the parking area, the three of us emerge from cover and block his path.

"Out of my way, kids. I'm in a hurry."

Malik raises the crowbar menacingly. "Sorry, mister. I need your van keys and your uniform."

He laughs. "No, seriously. I'm running a little late." His eyes narrow as he recognizes us. "Hey, you were in the Bearclaw yesterday. What do you want?"

Malik rears back the crowbar like a baseball bat. "I already told you. Your keys and your uniform. I don't want to have to hurt you."

The man steps forward, and tries to shove Malik out of his way. But Malik doesn't shove so easily, and stands his ground.

Amber speaks up. "Don't you get it, George? He's going to crack your skull open!"

George continues walking. "Let him try." He's getting angry now, and he doesn't look even a little bit scared.

Malik *does* look scared, the crowbar still cocked back, ready for a home run swing. "You crazy idiot, why are you making me do this? Don't you know who I am? I'm Gus Alabaster!"

George stops to stare at him. "The *gangster*? You're bat-poop crazy, that's who you are!"

Malik's eyes bulge. His whole body tenses for action like a panther ready to spring. I experience an instant of horror in that split second before the killer blow.

It doesn't happen. Instead, Malik drops the crowbar and enfolds the postal worker in a wrestling hug. George struggles against him, but Malik is just as big as he is, and strong. The man's arms are imprisoned at his side.

"The keys!" Malik grunts, the color of his face deepening through red into purple.

"It's a crime to interfere with the post office!"

Amber snatches up the fallen crowbar, steps back, and takes aim at the guy's head. The sheer determination in her eyes tells me one thing: maybe Malik won't do it, but she will.

I jump in front of her. *"No!"*

Her expression is stone cold. "You don't make a threat if you're not prepared to carry it out!"

"Hold him still!" I bellow at Malik. I reach down to poor George, and feel around his throat, looking for a certain pressure point. When I find it, I pinch hard. George's struggles die down and, in a couple of seconds, he slumps in Malik's arms, unconscious.

Malik is horrified. "What did you do? Is he dead?"

"No, he's just out cold. I couldn't let her brain him!"

Amber drops the crowbar. "Where'd you learn that, Eli?" she asks, impressed.

“It’s on the internet! There’s this artery, and when you cut off the blood flow—”

Malik interrupts. “Help me get his shirt off! Come on! We’re running out of time!”

Working as quickly as we can, we get the post office uniform off George and onto Malik. It’s a little loose, especially the pants. But Malik will be behind the wheel of the van when the Kefauver sentries see him, with his lower half out of view.

The car keys are in the pants pocket. I place Malik’s discarded things over the body of the unconscious George so he’ll have something to wear when he comes to.

“That’s my favorite T-shirt,” Malik says wistfully.

We’re into the van, down the road, and gone. 1:56.

As we pass the Tumbleweed Inn, Malik slows down so we can hop out. He drives on to Kefauver, tires squealing.

Amber and I run for the hotel.

Next stop: the computer room.

26

HECTOR AMANI

Turns out C. J. Rackoff is allergic to peanut butter. Who knew? And I love peanut butter. So I guess DNA doesn't mean everything.

It's an easy fix in the plan. Tori and I eat the PBJs, and leave the cheese sandwiches for "Uncle C.J." What's on the menu isn't the important thing anyway.

Rackoff washes his last bite down with a swig of lemonade, steps away from the picnic table bench, and collapses to the grass, grabbing at his throat.

Tori screams.

"*Uncle C.J.!*" I holler.

We kneel over him. "Get help! Our uncle's sick!" I yell up at the sentry in the tower.

The call for help turns out to be unnecessary. Three

other guards are racing toward us, proving that our private picnic wasn't so private after all.

"Allergies!" Rackoff rasps. "Peanuts! Throat closing up!"

Nobody waits for a gurney. Two of the officers grab him by the legs and under the arms, and run into the building. We follow. He's our uncle, after all. We're terrified—although not because of any allergy.

To our immense relief, they use a passkey to summon the emergency elevator. That means their destination is the second-floor hospital, which is exactly where we need Rackoff to be.

"Go to the security desk, and they'll see you out," one of the men advises.

"We're not leaving our uncle!" Tori sobs. Her ability to cry on cue is actually kind of impressive.

"He'll be well looked after," the other guard promises.

"No!" she shrieks. "We're staying with Uncle C.J.!"

The first man seems to weigh the need to get rid of us against the urgency of taking Rackoff to medical attention. When the elevator arrives, we're allowed to get on with them. "Stay close," he advises. "It's not safe for you to be wandering around without supervision."

The next time the doors open, we're in the hospital. It's

the one place inside Kefauver that doesn't look like a jail. It's white and clean with a sharp antiseptic smell, and the nurses and doctors are not in Department of Corrections uniforms. It reminds me of Dr. Bruder's clinic back in Serenity, only a lot bigger.

They load Rackoff onto a gurney, and give him a shot to counteract the allergy. Then they wheel him behind a portable partition to wait for the doctor. The guards try to take us out of there, but Tori pitches an absolute fit, screaming, *"Not till I know he's going to be okay!"*

For a minute, I'm afraid the guards are going to overrule us. But before they can, the nurse relents. "The doctor will be a few more minutes. Let them keep their uncle company. It could help his breathing if he's relaxed. Have a heart. They're just kids."

That's how we end up all alone with C. J. Rackoff behind the partition.

Tori does the scouting through the curtain. "Okay," she whispers, "the laundry chute is about thirty feet down the hall. Once you drop down there, you're in the prison laundry, right next door to the workshop."

"So what are we waiting for?" asks Rackoff.

I check my watch. "It's not time yet. At exactly two-oh-five, Eli hacks into the hospital computer and plants a notation that you've recovered, and been taken back to your cell."

He seems impressed. "Old Felix picked some choice DNA when he built his clone army."

I think that's supposed to be a compliment.

But there's not much time to be insulted. At 2:04, we roll the gurney through the curtain.

And freeze.

There's a guard in the hall, not six feet from the chute. We pull Rackoff back behind the partition. I turn to Tori and mouth the words: *Do they know?*

She shakes her head, directing me to peer through the gap in the hanging fabric. The guard is laughing with one of the nurses, showing her something on his phone. Okay, so they aren't onto us, but this could be just as bad. I glance at my watch. It's 2:06. Eli has already done his thing on the computer. We're ready to go! But how can we dump someone down the laundry chute with two people standing *right there*?

Rackoff regards us questioningly. Tori silences him with a finger to her lips. Her expression says it all: not a sound. This is deadly serious.

The minutes pass like months. 2:07 . . . 2:08. Beads of sweat are forming on her brow. Throughout the preparation, the one thing she impressed on us over and over again was split-second timing. The computer hack, the laundry chute—bang, bang. It had to be that quick.

2:09 . . . 2:10. Who knows how this might throw off Malik in the USPS truck? The whole plan could fall apart!

Suddenly, Tori squeezes my arm hard enough to splinter bone. The guard and the nurse are starting away. I begin a mental ten count to make sure they're gone, but Tori springs into action before I get to eight. She blasts out of the partition, pushing the gurney ahead of her. I scramble to catch up.

A final scan to confirm the coast is clear, and I open the chute. It's the work of seconds for Rackoff to roll off the stretcher and wriggle feet first into the passage, for all the world like a little kid going down a slide at the park.

We hear a distant *foomp,* the sound of him hitting a laundry bin one floor below.

The next part we can only imagine: Rackoff scrambling out of the laundry, and slipping into the workshop next door. There are guards down there, and getting caught is always a possibility. But he's a familiar face, wearing the same prison fatigues as everybody else. So there's no reason he can't blend in with the other prisoners on detail there. Anyway, it's out of our hands now. Our last remaining job is to get ourselves out of Kefauver.

We walk briskly to the nurse's station. Tori says, "We're ready to leave now."

The nurse looks surprised. "What about your uncle?"

"He got better," she says, "so they took him back to his cell."

Frowning, she checks the computer. "So they did."

Good old Eli!

Tori's eyes brim with tears. "We haven't seen him in so long!"

She's such a good actress that I almost cry myself.

"I'm sorry." She hands us each a pass and points us in the direction of the elevator. "Show these to the sentry downstairs, and they'll escort you to the front gate."

We step onto the elevator. We feel relief that our part is over. But it's dwarfed by the understanding that so much can still go wrong.

Now it's all up to Malik.

27

MALIK BRUDER

If we ever manage to make a real life for ourselves, remind me never to get a job working for the post office. The uniforms are itchy.

But I'm glad I've got that sucker on when I roll up to the front gate of Kefauver.

The sentry peers in at me. I can't help noticing the rifle strapped to his back. "Where's George?"

I keep the hat pulled low over George's mirrored sunglasses, and speak in my deepest voice. "He's got a pinched nerve in his neck," I say, and almost laugh in spite of how scared I am. There's not much Gus Alabaster in me right now. Or maybe the problem is my butt hurts from sitting on a postal manual of US ZIP codes so I'll look taller. The metal rings of the binding are digging into my skin, but I'm afraid to shift to a more comfortable position.

They open up the back of the truck to make sure I'm not smuggling anything inside. It's empty, as it's supposed to be. That's the way it works—empty going in, loaded with brand-new mail sacks going out. Or, in the case of today, loaded with mail sacks plus one sleazy embezzler.

As I'm passed through the security gates, I reflect that C. J. Rackoff can't be all bad because, without his DNA, there could never be Hector. I'm still blown away by the fact that we actually got Hector back, that the shrimp is alive and well, and with us. When I think about the days when we believed he was dead, it still casts a dark shadow over me.

Concentrate! I admonish myself. *There will be plenty of black clouds to go around if you screw this up!*

A signalman waves me over, directing me toward a loading bay. I experience a moment of genuine alarm. Frieden and I have been driving for so long that we've started to forget the fact that we're basically faking it, and have very few driving skills at all. I don't really know how to back up a car, much less a huge cargo van. If I bash in a part of their prison, they're going to want to take a closer look at this young employee the post office sent to fill in for George.

So I back it up, because I've got no choice, inching along

at a snail's pace. Meanwhile, I check my mirrors, waiting for the screech of metal that will tell me and the world that I've blown it for everybody.

It doesn't come. I'm in!

I jump out of the van and run to open the rear doors. My eyes pan the workshop—dozens of inmates, all dressed in the same orange jumpsuit Rackoff was wearing yesterday. There are guards, too, with that blank look they have. Like they could just as easily shake your hand or shoot you through the head—it makes no difference to them. And mailbags. George was right. If this is a day's output, how could one country possibly need so many? Seriously, the postmaster general must be eating them! They've got haystacks of them loaded up on wooden skids, and the prisoners are securing them in place with plastic wrap that they're unwinding from giant rolls.

I scan the faces sticking out of the bright orange collars. No Rackoff. Where is the guy? Did something go wrong? Was he caught? Hector and Tori were only taking him as far as the laundry chute. He had to make it the rest of the way here on his own. Let's face it, he has the same DNA as Hector. I love the kid, but I wouldn't trust him to cross a room without tripping over his own feet.

A forklift picks up the first skid and places it inside the

van. My lunch is rising. There are two more to go, and then what? I'm going to have to drive out, whether I have Rackoff or not.

The second skid is wrapped and loaded. Oh no! Feverishly, my mind goes over every detail of our plan. What am I missing? Is there something I should be doing?

The third and final skid is wrapped. The forklift picks it up.

Don't just stand there! I want to scream at myself. *Can't you see it's all going down the toilet? Do something!* But there's nothing to do. I'm not a magician. I can't conjure Rackoff out of no Rackoff.

Agony. There's no other word for it as I watch the skid arcing past me toward the last space in the van's cargo hold. It's not just a load of jail-made mailbags; it's a ticket for eleven clones to be able to prove who they are, and what's been done to them. And maybe, just maybe, have a future!

I'm staring at this last skid, struggling to keep myself from howling in frustration, and that's when I see it. Buried in the beige of the burlap is—a knee?

There's someone hiding in there!

And my next thought: *Rackoff!*

He must have taken off the bright orange jumpsuit to avoid being spotted when he crawled in under the skid of mailbags. Then he let himself be wrapped up into the shipment, and loaded into my van!

For a moment, I'm overcome with admiration.

As soon as the forklift withdraws, I'm about to slam the rear doors shut when a guard stops me.

"Not so fast."

Did he see? Does he know?

He turns to the assembled prisoners and barks, "Head count!"

I tremble through that count but, miraculously, they have the correct amount of guys. Rackoff isn't on work detail; he's supposed to be having a picnic with his niece and nephew. So how could he be missing?

Now that I have the okay, I close up the van, jump behind the wheel, and drive off. My biggest effort is not to floor it. They'll get suspicious if I leave the building at a hundred miles an hour.

"Mr. Rackoff?" I call over my shoulder.

"Keep your big mouth shut until we're past that gate," the skid replies.

Obviously, he's overcome with gratitude.

At the main sentry station, I hold my breath as they open the back doors and scan my cargo. If I caught a glimpse of a knee amid all those mail bags, maybe one of them can too. When the phone rings in the gatehouse, I almost launch myself through the roof of the van, positive they've discovered that Rackoff is missing. But all they say to me is, "Tell George to ice that neck." I promise to pass on the message. At this point, I'd promise them anything.

And then we're out. I can't describe the feeling. The craziest, most impossible million-to-one shot in history, and we pulled it off! I don't even know if Gus Alabaster could have done this. Or any of the other master criminals we're cloned from. This is big-time!

Rackoff seems to sense my triumph. "Congratulations, kid. You did good."

"Thanks!" I know he's a terrible person, but I'm so pumped up that I need to talk about it. Besides him, who can I ever tell and not get arrested? "So what are your plans once you get back out there in the world?"

A chuckle comes from the bundle. "I've got an iron or two in the fire. First things first, I've got to bust out of this shrink-wrap."

"We'll swing by the motel and pick up the others," I promise. "They'll get you out."

I turn into the Tumbleweed Inn, and cross the parking lot, bumping down to the hard-packed dirt as I pull behind Room 18. Their faces are already in the bathroom window, noses pressed to the glass. One by one, they climb out and cram themselves into the rear, where there's very little room.

"Where's Rackoff?" Hector asks, mystified.

"Down here," comes the reply. "Get me out of this gift basket. I'm suffocating."

We have to ditch the post office van as soon as possible. It's only a matter of time before the Kefauver authorities realize that we used it to break out one of their prisoners. Our plan is to go back to where we parked the pool/bean truck and continue on in that one.

As we drive, the others rip away the plastic wrap imprisoning Rackoff. Turns out the guy's wearing nothing but a pair of boxer shorts. Trust me, it's not a pleasant sight.

"I can't believe we did it," Eli says in an awed tone. "I mean, we must have always felt it was possible, or else we never would have tried. But the fact that we pulled it off just blows me away."

There's a chorus of agreement.

Tori is all business. "We're going to switch to a different truck that can't be so easily identified. We'll use that one for our getaway. Okay?"

"Okay." In the rearview mirror, I see Rackoff regard her with an inscrutable expression. "But I don't think it's going to work out like that."

And then I hear it—we all hear it—a rhythmic thrumming coming from outside. It's more than just sound. There's a vibration to it, one that you feel in the deepest reaches of your body. Just as it registers with me that the sensation is familiar, it happens.

The trees are buffeted by strong winds, and the wheel gets harder to manage in my hands. Up ahead in the road, a giant black military helicopter comes into view, settling down onto the roadbed, blocking our way. I slam on the brakes, and the van fishtails to a screeching, lurching halt. My passengers are bounced around like Ping-Pong balls.

That's not any chopper. That's—

"*Purples!*" wheezes Amber in horror.

A trap! The emotions flash through me, one after the other: shock . . . outrage . . . terror . . .

"*Get us out of here!*" barks Eli.

I'm way ahead of him. I throw the van into reverse and make a frantic three-point turn that almost sends us down an embankment. I stomp on the gas, and the van leaps forward, heading back in the direction of Kefauver. At this point, anything is better than Purple People Eaters.

Suddenly, there are two identical black SUVs coming at

us, one in each lane. There's no way around them. The road is completely blocked, a ditch on one side, the embankment on the other.

In the side mirror, I can already see men pouring out of the chopper. They're not wearing the purple uniforms; they're dressed in street clothes, but there's no mistaking their military posture and movements. These are the Purples, all right.

We're trapped.

What can I do? I stop.

"How did they find us?" Eli laments.

"Well, I guess you're not the masterminds everyone thinks you are," Rackoff drawls. "They drew you to me, with Hector's help, of course."

"Hector?" My head whips around to look at him.

Hector is red-faced and miserable. "You left me stranded in the woods! What choice did I have but to go back to Serenity and cut a deal? Catching you was the only bargaining chip I had! I'm sorry!"

I'm too stunned to be angry. Sold out—and by my best friend.

Rackoff slaps him hard across the face. "You have nothing to be sorry about! You did what you had to do to survive, just like I would have! We're the same person, you and me!"

"No!" Hector whimpers.

"It makes no sense!" Tori exclaims. "They've known where we are for a couple of days! Why wait till now to pick us up?"

"Don't you get it yet?" Rackoff asks in amusement. "First they had to use you to get me out of Kefauver. Who do you think has been bankrolling Project Osiris ever since Tamara Dunleavy dropped out? This escape has always been a part of that deal—fourteen years in coming, but well worth the investment."

They're pouring from the SUVs, too, now. Mostly Purples, but I recognize their ringleader, Felix Frieden, or Hammerstrom, or whatever his name is. And—yikes—it's my dad, Dr. Bruder. My burning desire to take his bow tie and shove it up his nose evaporates with an unexpected pang of regret at the sight of him: *He'd never hurt me. He loves me.*

"No!" I shout aloud, trying to shatter the thought.

There's a sharp banging on the rear doors.

"Open up!" barks Felix Frieden.

Eli blanches.

Not Laska, though. The more hopeless our situation

becomes, the more her jaw sticks straight out. She squats and struggles to lift up the heavy wooden skid that held the mail sacks and Rackoff.

"What are you doing?" Rackoff asks suspiciously.

"Maybe you're the one who's not such a mastermind," I sneer at him, bending my shoulder to give her a hand.

Growing up in Serenity, all Amber and I ever did was argue and insult each other. But these days, she's one of my favorite people. What do you do when you're hopelessly cornered and outnumbered? You fight that much harder—using every weapon at hand. And the fact that you can't win doesn't change anything.

Go, Laska! I should have appreciated you before it was too late.

Eli and Tori join us, and we heave the big skid upright. I reach for the door latch, but before I spring it, I turn to Hector.

"The next time you see me, you'd better be running the other way."

"I'm sorry, Malik!" he whimpers again.

"Not sorry enough, but you will be."

I pop the doors, and the four of us crash out of the van, pushing the skid in front of us into the mass of Purples and parents. It's a beautiful thing. We flatten everyone standing in the front ranks. A forest of grasping arms reaches for us, but somehow we avoid them, protected behind the heavy base like it's a tractor blade. My loving father jabs at me with a syringe filled with some kind of cloudy liquid. But he misses, and the wood strikes his shoulder, bouncing him out of the way. The syringe goes flying.

I've lost track of Tori, and a hand grabs Eli by the back of the collar, yanking him out of my line of vision. It's just Laska and me now, thrusting with all our might behind the skid, bulldozing like our lives depend on it, which they do.

All at once, the wood falls flat to the ground, and we see the slope in front of us, a steep embankment down to a river below. The base is already sliding on the incline.

"Come on!" Amber shouts, leaping onto it.

It's the craziest thing anybody's ever done. And, I realize, the only chance for at least two of us to get away. I hurl myself onto the wooden slats. The impact of my weight moves the skid even faster, taking us over the edge. There's a lot of shouting and running. The Purple we call Mr. Universe dives for the skid, and actually gets a grip on it for a second. But Amber kicks his hand away. And we're out of his reach, sliding down the slope, like we're on a toboggan ride over snow.

The acceleration is scary, and I understand immediately that when we reach the bottom, we'll either be free, or dead. Either way, we won't have to worry about the Purples we've just slipped away from.

"You're insane!" I scream at Amber.

"I know!" she shouts right back.

Watching her as the skid speeds up, blurring the world around us, it dawns on me that this girl has zero fear. Well, I've got enough for both of us. I wonder if Gus Alabaster was this scared through all the dangers he must have faced.

It's an interrupted thought, because that's when we reach the river. You normally consider water a soft landing. Maybe not in Texas. We hit the rushing stream like it's reinforced concrete. For a second, I'm airborne, launched clean off the slats. Then white water surrounds me, surging down my gasping throat, leaving me choking. I struggle to stay afloat, but I can't catch my breath. The eddying current drives me under.

All that water polo training, and I'm going to drown!

Even now, in the greatest panic I've ever experienced, I can't help but resent Happy Valley. Turns out, that stupid town will be the only life I'll ever know.

I surface, thrashing blindly, searching for a glimpse of wood. A hand comes out of nowhere, slapping me across the face.

Laska!

"What was that for?" I sputter.

"Shut up and hang on!"

She's in the water too, holding on to the skid with one hand and me with the other. The river washes us downstream at astonishing speed. All we can do is close our eyes and go with the flow. I'm underwater for at least two-thirds of the ride, sneaking a breath whenever I can. If it wasn't for Laska, I'd be fish food. But the current is taking us far away from the Purple People Eaters, and that's a good thing.

It feels like hours, although it's only a few minutes before the torrent calms down a little, and we're able to haul ourselves onto the skid, riding it like a raft. I get about thirty splinters. They hurt way less than the rest of me.

By unspoken agreement—because we're both too breathless to speak—we don't try for shore. Shore means Purples, who'll be coming after us. This river is like nature's getaway car. A gift.

Finally, I find my voice. "The others . . ."

"Caught," Amber manages to gasp. "They must be."

A wave of sympathy washes over me. Poor Frieden, poor

Torific. I'd love to believe otherwise, but I'd be a moron to deny the truth. We're on our own now.

If Project Osiris is ever going to be defeated, it'll be up to Amber and me.

28

ELI FRIEDEN

A rough hand grabs me from behind, strangling me with my own collar.

Tori! Where's Tori?

No time to worry about that now. The chokehold is so strong that my vision starts to cloud. I know I have mere seconds to remain conscious.

Desperately, I twist away from the grip, dropping to the gravel of the shoulder and rolling away onto the grass. I see the gray flannel of my attacker's slacks stepping toward me. I reach for something I can use to defend myself. A stick, a rock—anything.

My hand closes on a tubular object, smooth, cool, and plastic. I stare at it. A syringe. It was in Dr. Bruder's hands just a few seconds ago. He must have dropped it.

Wielding it like a knife, I get to my knees and stab it into my enemy's thigh. He stops dead, letting out a gasp of pain that's instantly familiar.

Dread washes over me. It's Felix Frieden.

My father's eyes widen. "Son—"

No! I will not let this monster control me again!

"I'm not your son!" I barely recognize my own voice. "Thanks to you, I'm not anybody's son!"

"Eli—" He takes one more step and collapses to the ground, out cold.

I look at the syringe in my hand. Only a tiny amount of its contents has been used. Dr. Bruder must have filled it with a powerful tranquilizer, intent on recapturing his clones without a fight.

A chorus of angry voices sounds. I wheel just in time to see Malik and Amber disappear down the embankment, sliding on the wooden skid. A stampede of Purples charges after them, slipping and sliding on the hill.

That's when I spy Tori, struggling against a Purple I recognize as Bryan Delaney, the husband of our water polo coach. I come up behind him and stab the needle into the back of his shoulder, depressing the plunger just a little. Bryan drops like a stone.

Yep—tranquilizer, definitely.

Tori grabs my arm and begins hauling me away from the embankment toward the helicopter. I see her plan immediately. With everyone freaking out over Malik and Amber, the chopper is sitting all alone on the road.

"I can't fly that thing!" I protest.

"But *he* can." She points to the bubble. The pilot is visible, sitting at the controls.

I must be stupid, because I can't follow her logic. "If I knock out the pilot, he can't fly it either!"

She looks exasperated. "A weapon is strongest when you *don't* use it. Threaten him."

We jump aboard, and Tori pulls the hatch shut behind us. The pilot starts to get up, and I brandish the syringe.

"This already took out two people, and see how much I've got left," I rasp. "Take off. Now."

He doesn't move, eyeing the needle fearfully.

I add, "They'll wake up eventually. But if I pump the rest of it into you, you never will."

Still he hesitates. I realize the flaw in Tori's strategy. I can't be bluffing. If he doesn't obey, I have to be willing to see it through.

My voice becomes low, flat, and the temperature of dry ice. "The guy I'm cloned from killed nine people. Want to be number ten?"

That does it. He manipulates the controls. The engine roars to earsplitting life. The rotor starts to turn, slowly at first, then picking up speed.

Through the Plexiglas, I see some of the Purples break off pursuit of Malik and Amber, and come running back in our direction.

I press the needle flat against the pilot's neck.

No words are needed. We lift off, hovering over the chaotic scene. Purples mill around in our windstorm, shouting up at us.

The radio crackles to life. *"What are you doing? Land that bird! Pronto!"*

In response, Tori pulls a metal first aid kit off a bulkhead bracket and smashes the transceiver until wires and pieces pop out in a puff of smoke. The speaker goes silent.

She drops the kit and points. "Look!" Far below, the wooden skid is rocketing down the river with two tiny figures dangling behind it. An instant later, they're out of sight, obscured by trees and terrain, surging toward an uncertain fate.

"Follow the river!" I order.

The pilot takes us out over the waterway. We peer down, hoping to catch a glimpse of our two friends through a gap in the foliage.

That's when we see the black SUVs speeding along the road, tailing us. My eyes meet Tori's. There's nothing we can do for Malik and Amber. We have to escape Project Osiris.

"Get us out of here," I tell the pilot.

"Which direction?"

"Doesn't matter. South."

We bank away through the sky, climbing higher and putting distance between ourselves and the SUVs. After a few minutes, we can no longer see them. The enemy is out of range, but so are our friends. We have no idea if Malik and Amber will be captured, or if they'll even survive the rage of the river.

We have no idea if we'll ever see them again.

The knot in my stomach tightens, and I bite the side of my mouth, hoping the pain will keep me focused. It's sad, but sadness is no reason to blow our only shot at freedom.

As we fly, I stay behind the pilot, holding the syringe against his neck, just as a reminder. That's probably what Bartholomew Glen would do, although he might be thinking up crossword puzzles to communicate his orders. I hate him, but I'm pretty sure that, without his DNA, we never could have made it this far, flying away from the trap Osiris set for us.

Tears are streaming down Tori's cheeks, but her expression remains calm and resolute. For sure it's the others on her mind—especially Amber. The two of them have always been closer than sisters.

"Maybe they're okay," I offer. I wish I could give her more, but I'm not even sure *we're* okay. We're away from the Purples now, but what about the pilot? Wherever we land, we'll be on foot, leaving a potential capturer equipped with a helicopter.

I know how Bartholomew Glen would solve that problem, but I refuse to be him.

We've been in the air about forty minutes when the pilot says, "Look, I've got to set her down."

I press down a little harder with the flat of the needle. "*We* decide when and where you land."

"No," he replies evenly. "The fuel tank decides." He indicates a gauge on the control panel. The indicator is already at E. "One way or another, we'll be on the ground in a few minutes. A very few."

I scan the horizon. There's a city up ahead—it's no Denver, but it's definitely a population center—large enough for two fugitive clones to disappear into. "What's that?"

"Lubbock," he replies.

"Can we make it?" asks Tori.

"On fumes, maybe."

Our eyes move back and forth between the fuel gauge and the approaching skyline of Lubbock, Texas. The engine coughs.

The pilot leans on the controls and we begin to descend.

"We're not there yet," I say harshly, wiggling the syringe to remind him that it's still there.

"You do what you've got to do," he tells me. "I'm doing what I've got to do."

The engine coughs again, shaking us. He's right. It's now or never.

We're still a few miles from Lubbock, above ranch country. It's a rough landing, and, like the pilot warned, probably on fumes. We drop the last few feet, landing with a crunch in a stubbly field. A crack appears in the Plexiglas, but otherwise the chopper is intact.

The pilot hunches over the controls, panting from the effort of bringing us in.

I say, "You'll wake up. I promise," and prick him with the needle, careful to inject only a small amount of tranquilizer into the back of his neck. "Sorry."

He's out cold even before I withdraw the syringe. Immediately, I drop it to the deck, not wanting it in my hand a split second longer than necessary.

Tori pops the hatch. We jump to the ground and start running. The only witnesses to our strange arrival and departure are a few dozen head of longhorn cattle in the next field.

There are questions to be asked: Where can we go? What can we do? But there's no time to think about that now. When the pilot regains consciousness, we have to be gone.

In spite of everything we've been through, we don't get tired. Our strides are powered by sheer desperation. The one thing we had on our side was the fact that the four of us were together. That's gone. And the hunters are close behind us.

I keep my eyes on the horizon—the future. We can get there; we can have one. We have skills locked in the DNA code of every cell in our bodies. We might not have discovered how to use them yet—not fully, anyway. But they have to be there.

We're masterminds.

Turn the page for a sneak peek
at the final book in the series:

MASTERMINDS
PAYBACK

1

AMBER LASKA

The branch comes out of nowhere.

I don't even see it until it's too late to shout a warning. One second, we're riding down the river. The next, the limb catches Malik on the side of the head, pitching him off our makeshift raft into the water.

I don't hesitate. I can't. The current is so fast that I could be a quarter-mile downriver before I make up my mind. And anyway, it's a pretty selfish move. I've already lost Eli and Tori. If I lose Malik, too, I'm all alone.

I hit the water with a splash, and begin to stroke upstream. It's a struggle with the river boiling all around me, and I'm grateful for the water polo training I got back in Serenity.

I never thought I'd be grateful for anything about growing up in that town.

Malik is moving toward me, carried by the current. He looks okay, except for a bloody gash behind his ear. I take hold of him in the classic Red Cross lifesaving position and swim for shore.

He's shouting something, but I can't make it out over the roar of the river. What's he saying?

"You idiot, Laska! What are you doing?"

"Rescuing you!" I snarl back.

"I don't need rescuing! Why'd you jump off the raft?"

He's struggling against my grip. I pull harder for the riverbank. "We're stronger when we stick together!"

"Don't give me that Serenity baloney. Now we're *both* going to get caught!"

He wrestles free of my grasp, and the two of us swim ashore. We crawl through the reeds onto dry land and lie side by side, gasping and glaring at each other. I'm twice as mad at him as he is at me, because I know that if he could catch his breath, he'd be yelling at me.

He's right about one thing, though. Getting caught is a real danger. The Purple People Eaters saw us ride off on the river. When you escape from a commando team, you have to figure they'll be coming after you. Soon.

We scurry through the cover of the trees, staying low. After ten minutes, we come upon a two-lane highway with dirt shoulders. I'm about to step out, but Malik pulls me back.

"Use your head," he hisses. "The next car around the bend could be one of their SUVs. I'm going up to see what I can see."

"Up?"

He starts climbing a huge old tree. I follow him. I've already jumped off a raft so I wouldn't be alone. I'm not about to stand there at the side of the road, waiting to get scooped up by Purples. It's a testament to what we've been through since escaping Serenity that neither of us thinks twice about scaling a thirty-foot oak. Running for your life does that to a person.

By the time we make it to the top, we wish we hadn't bothered. The two black SUVs carrying our pursuers are heading our way. They're hopscotching along the road, stopping periodically to send out teams of searchers into the woods. The lead car pulls over about three hundred yards short of us, and four men head into the trees.

We exchange a look of pure horror. Not only are they close, but we've trapped ourselves thirty feet in the air.

And then a pickup truck appears in the distance, coming

from the opposite direction, pulling a large white camper. It's going pretty fast, but it has to slow down to take the curve. In that instant, we both know what we're going to do. It's reckless and insane, but it's also our only option.

Malik is already hustling down to a lower branch, dragging me with him.

"I get it!" I whisper urgently. "Worry about yourself!"

About fifteen feet off the ground, a heavy branch extends out over the road. We crawl onto it, Malik in the lead. In a few seconds, the camper will pass directly beneath us.

"Jump early," I advise. "You know, to compensate for the motion of the—"

I never finish the sentence. He pushes me off the branch and lets go himself.

The drop is only about six feet, but it feels like a hundred miles. Maybe that's because, while we're falling, we have no idea if we're about to land catlike on the camper or with a splat on the pavement.

I hit the roof and flatten myself to the metal surface. Malik lands behind me a split second later. I look back with furious eyes.

He offers a slight shrug. "You said jump early."

I almost say, *I'm never going to forgive you for this!* I don't because this is at least the fifteenth thing I'm never going to forgive Malik for. Besides, he did care enough to push me, which means he's probably even more scared of being left alone than I am. Malik may look like a tough guy and a bruiser, but deep down, he's a big baby.

We stay pressed to the roof, keeping as low as possible, so we don't get to enjoy the moment when the camper sails by the SUVs. Too bad. I would have loved to laugh in their faces. Of course, that would have given us away. We have to be satisfied with the fact that they're going to search for hours, only to come up empty. I hope the mosquitoes are hungry tonight.

As the road straightens out, the camper speeds up again, and the wind begins to whip at our wet clothes. Suddenly, I'm freezing despite the heat, but that's far from the real issue. We're clinging to the roof like flies on a wall, with nothing to hang on to.

Malik inches his way up beside me. "Now what?" He has to shout to be heard over the wind and road noise.

"How should I know?" I shoot back. "This was your idea!"

"I only thought about getting away! I never made it this far!"

I look around. No luggage rack, no handhold, no bracing point. "Just hang on!" I manage.

In spite of everything we've been through, I've never been so scared in my life. Every curve threatens to hurl us off the camper. Every bump is sure to launch us into outer space. We lie flat, pressing our hands and feet against unyielding metal. Within minutes, our entire bodies ache with the effort. I'm a workout nut, but this is beyond anybody's physical capabilities.

Back in Serenity, I used to make a list every morning, planning out my entire day. If I could do that now, clinging to the roof in terror and agony, there would only be one item on it:

THINGS TO DO TODAY

- Don't let go!

The pickup just keeps driving, hauling our camper after it. It's putting miles between us and the Purples, but our daring escape isn't going to do us much good if we end up roadkill.

"I'm sorry!" Malik says suddenly.

"Huh?"

He's babbling now. "I'm sorry I made you jump! And—and for all that other mean stuff! If we get killed, you should know!"

Before I can reply, the truck's engine noise changes and we start to slow down. I dare to raise my head and see a weather-beaten old gas station coming up on the right.

"We're stopping!" I exclaim emotionally. I honestly don't believe we could have held on much longer.

"I was starting to think this bonehead was going camping in Oregon," Malik adds, sounding more like his old self.

The tires crunch as we pull off the road onto the gravel drive and come to a stop at the gas pump. The driver gets out of the pickup and heads around the back of the minimart to the restroom.

Malik and I don't wait for an engraved invitation. We crawl to the back of the camper and climb down the ladder. My arms are pure pain from shoulder to fingertips. When my feet touch the ground, I'm amazed that my rubbery legs hold me upright.

"I accept your apology," I whisper.

"What apology?" he growls. "Come on!"

We start for the cover of the wooded area behind the station when Malik suddenly freezes in front of the minimart. I look back to see what has captured his attention.

He's standing opposite a newspaper box, staring at a copy of today's *Dallas Morning News.* The headline is something about global warming, but I skip down the page to the story that's caught his eye:

GUS ALABASTER RELEASED FROM PRISON ON COMPASSIONATE GROUNDS

I recognize the name instantly, and just as instantly, I understand Malik's fascination with the news.

Gus Alabaster is one of the most notorious gangsters in American history.

He's also the criminal mastermind Malik is cloned from.

2

ELI FRIEDEN

Nice bracelet. Gold, studded with glittering stones.

"No price tag," I observe.

"Those are diamonds, Eli," Tori tells me. "Diamonds are expensive. Besides, check out how they've placed it in the display case. You can tell it's the star of the show. I wonder what it's worth."

I peer closer, my nose touching the hot glass of the jewelry store window. I'm not worried about attracting attention. The store is closed, and there's hardly anybody around. It's a broiling afternoon in Amarillo, Texas—the kind where sensible people stay inside in the air-conditioning. Our long bus ride north from Lubbock didn't buy us cooler weather.

I get what Tori's saying. It's like all the other pieces

are in orbit around that one bracelet. I'm not surprised she noticed. She has a great eye for detail that made her the best artist in our hometown, Serenity, New Mexico. I'm also not surprised that she zeroed in on the item in the whole shop that would be most valuable to someone who steals it.

That comes from a part of Tori neither of us wants to think about.

To be honest, it all looks pretty expensive to me—rings, necklaces, earrings, and brooches; gold, platinum, gemstones. Not that we ever learned much about money in Serenity. Our parents took care of that, and they always seemed to have plenty. That was before we found out the whole town was fake, and the fakest thing about it was our parents. The creepy truth: they're scientists who've been studying us since the day we were born.

Of course, since leaving Serenity, we've learned a lot about money. Like you really can't survive without it. And we're running out of what little we had in the first place.

"No point wasting our time wondering how much we could get for a bracelet we're never going to touch in the first place." I point to a sign in the window: *THESE PREMISES PROTECTED BY APEX SECURITY.*

She steps back, scanning the store. When Tori looks at something, she takes in every detail, almost like she's inhaling it. "Well, the alarm wires go through the door." Then she points to a window in the second floor of the strip mall shop. "But I bet there's a way in through the attic."

"The store has motion sensors," I point out.

It stops her for a second but not much longer. "See the mail slot in the door? If we put a bird in through there —"

"You want to catch a bird?"

"I'm just thinking out loud. My mind does that on its own. Doesn't yours?"

Well, yeah, but not like Tori's. Nobody's mind works like Tori's. Okay, scratch that. Maybe one other person's—and she's in jail right now.

"Anyway," she goes on, "the bird sets off the motion sensor and triggers the alarm. But when the police come, they see it's just a bird. So the owner turns off the motion sensor until he can come back in the morning and chase the bird out. And we have all night to get in from the upstairs. Simple."

I stare at her—but it isn't Tori that I see. It's a convicted bank robber named Yvonne-Marie Delacroix, presently serving a life sentence in a Florida prison. Tori is an exact copy of her, right down to the DNA in every one of her cells. Tori has never robbed a bank in her life. Still, you have to figure that everything Yvonne-Marie is capable of, Tori could be too.

"But we're not going to do that, right?" I say anxiously.

I have to ask, because I'm like Tori—I have the DNA of a criminal too. Not a bank robber. That would be a huge upgrade for me. But we've been breaking the law a lot lately. Don't get me wrong; we didn't bust out of Serenity to go on a crime spree. It's more like it took a crime spree to escape Serenity. And to keep us from getting caught and dragged back there.

Suddenly, Tori points. "Heads up!"

Across the parking lot, the front sliding doors of the supermarket part to reveal an elderly lady pushing a heavily loaded grocery cart.

Tori's off like a shot, but I'm right behind her. "It's *my* turn!" I hiss.

"It's *my* turn!"

"No way. You got the fat guy in the cowboy hat, remember?"

Tori backs off, and I approach the old woman just as she pops the cargo door of a Buick SUV.

"Here, ma'am, let me help you with that." I grab a bag and load it into the back of the Buick.

She beams at me. "Well, aren't you sweet!"

I'm not even a little bit sweet. I am an exact genetic

match for Bartholomew Glen, California's notorious Crossword Killer. But on a ninety-eight-degree day, anyone who carries your parcels counts as sweet.

She tips me a dollar. A dollar! It would take more than a dollar's worth of soap and water just to wash the sweat off my poor sweltering body. I straggle back to Tori and we compare our take for the day.

"Fourteen dollars and fifty cents," I announce with a sigh. "For four hours in a parking lot."

"That bracelet could get us more," Tori puts in. "Then we could afford a hotel room. With real beds. And a bathroom."

"We're not criminals!"

"We kind of are," she reasons.

"Just because we're cloned from criminals doesn't mean we did any of the stuff they're in jail for," I insist.

That's what Serenity, New Mexico, turned out to be—not an actual town where people live and work and raise their kids, but a front for a twisted experiment called Project Osiris. Basically, the idea of Osiris is nature versus nurture. If you take evil people, raise them in the perfect community, and give them the perfect life, will they still turn out evil, because that's their nature? Or will they end up good, because that's how you've nurtured them to be?

You have to start an experiment like that from the very beginning, which means what you need is evil *babies*. Project Osiris cloned DNA samples from the worst criminal masterminds in the prison system and created us—exact copies of the scum of the earth. And they raised us as human guinea pigs to see if we could rise above our horrendous genes.

There are eleven of us, but only five escaped Serenity. One of us already turned out to be a traitor. Thanks to Hector Amani, we were almost recaptured four days ago. Tori and I got away by the skin of our teeth. The last we saw of Malik and Amber, they were being washed down white water by a brutal current. Even if they survived the river, they would have been in no shape to get away from their pursuers—our Serenity parents and their hired muscle, who we nicknamed the Purple People Eaters.

So it's up to us to stop Project Osiris. As tempting as it is to disappear and try to make new lives for ourselves, we can't turn our backs on the past. Six of our fellow clones are still under Osiris's thumb, with no idea of the truth about themselves. They're never far from our thoughts. When you grow up in such a tiny, isolated place, the handful of other kids in town are practically your brothers and sisters.

It seems impossible. I'm thirteen and Tori's only twelve.

Plus our story sounds totally nuts. How do we prove what's been done to us? Serenity's now a ghost town, all the evidence of the experiment burned to ashes.

The supermarket doors hiss open once more and a man steps out into the heat, struggling with two big bags.

Tori is already on the move. "My turn," she tosses over her shoulder at me.

I watch her catch up with the guy and take the bigger parcel from him—he won't let her carry both. They walk to his car, chatting amiably.

Tori loads the groceries into the man's trunk and he hands her a tip. The grin on her face is all the more remarkable because there's been so little to smile about these days. She pockets the bill and flashes me an open hand. That means five dollars, our biggest score of the day. I'm kind of insulted that nobody ever gives me that much. I guess Tori's a little stronger on charm than I am. That might be because her fake parents genuinely loved her—not like my dad, the ringleader of Osiris, who never had any use for me except as a lab rat.

A long dark sedan cruises across the blacktop and screeches to a halt right in front of Tori. The passenger door is flung open and a tall man wearing a black suit and sunglasses jumps out and grabs for her.

Too late the warning is torn from my throat. “Tori—run!”

She has another idea. She reaches into the grocery bag, pulls out a glass jar of pickles, and swings it at her attacker, catching him full in the face. He staggers back, dazed, his sunglasses askew. The pickle jar drops to the pavement and shatters.

I’m running flat out, desperate to reach her, my mind spinning with the horrible thought that Osiris has found us again. I don’t recognize the man in sunglasses, but he could easily be one of the Purples.

“What do you think you’re doing?” The shocked grocery shopper steps protectively in front of Tori.

The sedan’s driver leaps out and shoves him to the pavement with a warning of, “Mind your own business, old man!”

Tori reaches into the trunk for another weapon. This time, she’s not as lucky as she was with the pickle jar. She comes up with a long baguette and swings it like a baseball bat at the driver. With a cruel laugh, he allows her to club him with it a couple of times before yanking it from her hands.

Out of options, Tori flees. The driver springs after her. She’s the fastest and most athletic of us—burglar

DNA—and I toy with the possibility that she can outrun him. He's got long legs, though, every stride of his matching two of hers. He's gaining fast.

I've got to help her, but what can I do? I'm fifty feet behind, and slower than both of them.

And then it comes to me—the sedan is just standing there with the motor idling and both doors open!

I jump in and throw the car in gear. I've driven before—Malik and I both taught ourselves so we could escape from Serenity. I'm just about to take off after them when a hand reaches across the front seat and grabs at my elbow. I forgot about the other guy—the one Tori hit with the pickle jar. His sunglasses are broken, and a big angry bruise is blooming in the center of his forehead.

I stomp on the accelerator and yank the wheel hard left. The car bursts forward, swerving violently. I feel the grip release from my arm, and when I glance over at my attacker, he's not there anymore. He's in the rearview mirror, twenty feet behind, still rolling on the blacktop.

Ahead, the first guy is almost up to Tori, so close he could grab her at any second. I roar alongside them, yelling through the open passenger door. *"Get in!"*

READ THEM ALL!

"A thrilling and fun series perfect for middle grade adventure seekers."

—*School Library Journal*

An Imprint of HarperCollins*Publishers*

www.harpercollinschildrens.com